AN UNSEEN MENACE
SHADOWED MELINDA
MARSTON, THREATENING
HER REPUTATION, HER
SANITY - - AND HER LIFE!

Recently acquitted of murder, Melinda sought refuge in Mystic Manor, a gloomy old castle belonging to the regal Mrs. Jager. There she hoped to find peace and escape from the scorn of the villagers who still believed Melinda guilty.

But Melinda found Mystic Manor no haven, for even there a series of unexplained events occurred. Once again, Melinda's reputation was at stake, and not even Mrs. Jager could help her.

Melinda was determined to prove her innocence— even at the risk of her life. She traced the hidden menace to a ruined chapel on the grounds of Mystic Manor. Though the chapel was supposed to be abandoned, what she saw there struck fear in her heart.

THE SECRET OF HER TERROR LAY WITHIN THE EERIE CHAPEL. DARE MELINDA ENTER —PERHAPS NEVER TO LEAVE ALIVE?

MYSTIC MANOR

By Dorothy Daniels

Writing as Helen Gray Weston

WARNER

PAPERBACK LIBRARY
NEW YORK

WARNER PAPERBACK LIBRARY EDITION

First Printing: May, 1966
Second Printing: March, 1970
Third Printing: August, 1972

Warner Paperback Library is a division of Warner Books, Inc., 315 Park Avenue South, New York, N.Y. 10010.

ONE

The agony had been with me all day, but it was going to get worse when I left the graveside and walked between the rows of people to Dr. Bruce Erskine's carriage. Almost everyone in the town of Germond Hill had attended Vincent Seaton's funeral.

There were three reasons for such a lavish attendance. Vincent had been head schoolmaster of the town, a most handsome man, and a witty one. He dressed in the latest of styles and the male fashions of 1890 had scarcely been known in the village until he arrived.

Secondly, Vincent had been murdered and murder always draws a crowd of the morbidly curious. Third—I was going to be present and everyone wanted to see how I'd act. I had no doubt but that more than two-thirds of those present still believed I had killed Vincent. All of them, to the last man and woman, knew I'd been in love with him. Perhaps they expected that I'd faint, or possibly cry out my guilt, or even run madly from the scene.

I did none of those things. I dressed in black out of respect for the deceased, even if I had not respected him alive. I had ridden in the funeral carriage behind the hearse alone, for Vincent had no kin and the place of dubious honor was granted me by the trick of some macabre jokester.

I had remained dry-eyed, in full control of my emotions. Others broke down. I wasn't the only woman in Germond Hill who had loved Vincent, openly or secretly.

Dr. Bruce Erskine didn't arrive until the service was nearly ended. My head was lowered as the minister intoned a final prayer, yet without even glancing up to see who had taken a place beside me, I knew it was the good doctor. I sensed his comforting presence and I felt sustained by it. As the service ended, he took my arm, pressing it gently, as if by doing so he was telling me not to be frightened, for indeed I had reason to be.

I turned obediently and began to walk the gauntlet of cold stares. I kept my head high and my steps were steady. Had someone called out a derogatory word, or an accusa-

5

tion, I might have broken down, but all were grimly silent and by their silence they shouted their condemnation of me. The hearse, with its four black, plumed horses, was already leaving. We reached Bruce's carriage and he helped me onto the seat. He was beside me a moment later and he snapped the reins smartly. We moved off and the tension behind us was broken as everyone headed for their own conveyances, or the hired hacks which had brought them here.

The stares I glimpsed out of the corner of my eyes were hostile, more so than they might ordinarily have been because I was not being punished in any way. In fact, it must have seemed to these good people that I was actually being rewarded.

My hopes of getting away from the cemetery without incident were much higher than I'd expected. The carriage was moving; there was nothing anyone could do now.

Then the ludicrous figure in the threadbare black suit, black shirt and black stocking cap, worn even though it was summer and the day was hot, darted out before the horses, waving his skinny arms and shrieking like a madman which, in fact, he likely was. Billy Cornell was the town fool, the addlebrained simpleton who got along somehow without working very much. The man everyone laughed at because he didn't mind it, and the more they laughed, the more foolish he became. I'd always felt pity for him and whenever he approached me, I'd shown him only kindness.

There was, however, nothing foolish in what he did now. It was a determined, vicious attempt to frighten the pair of spirited horses pulling our carriage. Bruce wasn't the kind of man who became upset. Billy Cornell had picked the wrong victim this time. Bruce's pull tightened on the reins, holding the horses in check. When Billy furiously tried to pull at the harness as the carriage began to pass him, and the horses, terrified, started to rear, Bruce cut at him with the whip and it lashed him across the face, sending him screaming in pain off the cemetery roadway until he stumbled against an old gravestone and fell down.

"Now what made him do that?" Bruce asked, dismayed at what he'd been forced to do. "He's a fool, but never have I seen him display maliciousness before."

"He believed Vincent was his friend," I said.

6

"I see. And of course he blames you for Vincent's death."

"Yes, Doctor," I replied. "So does everyone else."

"Not everyone," he said.

"I'm sorry. Of course you're the exception. You and your very kind aunt. Had it not been for her, I don't know what I'd have done. I'm extremely fortunate to have two people who believe me innocent of the crime."

We passed beyond the limits of the graveyard and headed out along the road toward Mystic Manor, where I would make my home, at least temporarily, with Delphine Jager, Dr. Bruce Erskine's enormously rich aunt.

"May I ask you a very personal question, Melinda?"

I glanced at him and nodded. I knew what the question would be and I didn't blame him for asking it.

"Were you really in love with Vincent Seaton?"

"I thought I was. He had a way of making a girl believe he was completely and thoroughly in love with her."

"In your case, could it have been the truth?" Bruce suggested.

"No," I replied. "I returned to the schoolroom one evening for some papers which I had forgotten. He was there, with one of the girls from the village. I heard voices in his office and, curious, I went there. He was making love to a girl, using the same phrases to express it as he had to me. His voice was just as tender and, I might add, just as impassioned. Fortunately, I hadn't allowed him to turn my head as he had other young girls."

"When did you become acquainted with him?"

I knew Bruce, in his skilled manner, was urging me to talk, to ease the tension and nervousness which had built up in me at the ordeal I had just gone through.

"You see, though my father died two years ago, Mama's only been gone five months. They had provided me with a fine education so that I easily qualified as a schoolteacher. But, at Mama's death, I learned how destitute we really were. There was nothing left beyond what it required to bury her. I needed work quickly. I went to an agency which placed teachers and found there was little demand for them at mid-term. Then Vincent Seaton came by this office while I was there and asked for a teacher. They let him interview almost twenty young women and he chose me, even though I had no experience."

"I rather think I know why too," Bruce said.

7

"So do I—now. I had no kinfolk, nowhere to go and I needed the work badly. That gave him an opportunity to claim my gratitude and to make love to me at once. I'd never been in love. I'm but nineteen now. He swept me off my feet. I came here and worked under him. I think I did well with the children and I loved teaching. Vincent saw to it that the town provided me with a little house in which to live. But it didn't take me long to realize that Vincent was making love to any female who would listen to his blandishments, and when I was sure of this, I ordered him from my home. He argued with me, denying his philanderings. It made me angry because I had proof. I become so angry I lost my temper to the extent I shouted at him, I'm afraid. We were overheard quarreling. I couldn't deny that. The next day Vincent was found dead at my front door, shot through the chest. I was immediately arrested and, quite likely, convicted in the minds of the people of Germond Hill."

We were now riding close by the west bank of the Hudson River. Soon we'd begin the climb to the hill on top of which his aunt's castle-like home had been built. I had never ceased to marvel at the beauty of this Hudson Valley country and not even the tribulations I had just endured made the countryside any less beautiful to me.

"In time," Bruce said, "the good people of the village will realize you were innocent. Even if they don't find the real murderer, they'll understand that you couldn't have killed him. The gun with which he was shot was never found. Secondly, he had not been shot near your little cottage, but a considerable distance away, because he died from loss of blood actually, and there was little blood on your porch."

"Had it not been for you and Mr. Todd, the lawyer, I should very likely go on trial for murder in a few days. Instead, I am on my way to work for your aunt. My gratitude, Dr. Erskine, knows no bounds. I shall be forever indebted to you and to Mrs. Jager."

"It's a strange thing," he said with a frown. "I didn't suggest Aunt Delphine help you. She came to that decision by herself. It pleased me because, while I may be her nephew, I have always regarded her as a rather selfish woman with little thought or consideration for others. She must have been impressed with the unfairness of what hap-

8

pened to you. At any rate, you have a position that pays even more than teaching school did."

As he spoke, I studied him somewhat covertly. He was not a handsome young man, in the manner that Vincent had been. Vincent had a god-like head, thick blond hair that curled slightly, the brightest of blue eyes and a ready, pleasing smile, even if it was actually as false as his heart.

Dr. Bruce Erskine, on the other hand, was taller and sturdier than Vincent had been. His hair was a dark brown and his eyes were gray and serious, never mocking as Vincent's had so often been. Vincent had given the impression of grace, an Apollo, while Bruce suggested strength and power.

He was a very good doctor, I knew—a graduate of Harvard Medical School and well-versed in the art of healing. He would have been successful even if his aunt hadn't been one of the wealthiest women in the state.

The fact that he had chosen to practice in this little village instead of a large city where he could command much larger fees was further proof to me of his goodness. The fact that he was comfortably situated didn't enter into it. He might well have preferred a practice where his clients were members of high society. Certainly, with his manner, he would have been an instant success. Instead, he chose to minister to the villagers who were mostly of modest means and much more likely to pay their fees in poultry or vegetables from their gardens or freshly baked bread from their wives' kitchens. Yes, I had placed Bruce Erskine on a pedestal and I knew nothing or no one would ever topple him. Nor should anyone ever dare.

"What is it like at Mystic Manor?" I asked. "I've heard the village stories that a hundred people can be accommodated there."

Bruce's laugh was good-humored. "Well, not a hundred, though it is a historical fact that the Spanish Ambassador once paid a visit here with a retinue of forty and they were put up with no crowding or inconvenience. Frankly, I don't know how many rooms there are in the old place, but I should judge about sixty."

"What in the world are all those rooms used for?"

"Not much, these days. Aunt Delphine doesn't entertain on a scale comparable to that of her ancestors. Oh, there are formal dinners and dances now and then. Everybody had a suite of two rooms; there are servants quarters. I have a studio. . . ."

"I've heard you are a remarkably good artist," I said.

"Art is a hobby of mine. I don't try to make money at it, but I do love to paint. I should very much like to paint your portrait one day soon, if you will permit me."

"My portrait?" I asked, and I knew full well I was blushing furiously. "Why, Dr. Erskine, why should you wish to paint me?"

"Because you're a very attractive girl, that is why," he said. "Melinda, you're actually a beautiful girl. There's gold in your hair and interesting flecks of darker blue in your regularly blue eyes. You have the round face of youth, a very pretty nose and a smooth chin line. I would say you'd be a fine subject."

"You may paint me if you like," I said. "It's flattering to be asked."

"Good. We'll make the arrangements after you find out what you have to do and how many hours your duties require. Offhand, I should say you'll have plenty of time on your hands. Being social secretary to a woman who leads absolutely no social life can't take up much time."

"Your aunt explained to me about that," I said. "I am to be the secretary of Charity, her sister, but part of my duties will be to see if I can bring her among people more often. I take it she's shy."

"Very much so. There are times when days go by that she doesn't even leave her rooms. Whenever Aunt Delphine gives a social affair and Charity can't avoid attending, she suffers no end. Perhaps you'll be good for her. Aunt Delphine loves her very much—she's Delphine's younger sister, you understand."

"Yes, I was told so, Doctor."

"Charity won't be hard to handle, but my own younger sister, Fern, isn't going to like you."

"In heaven's name, why not? I haven't even met her. . . ." I began to protest.

"That matters not at all, Melinda. Fern is an attractive girl, but not nearly as pretty as you. She's going to resent that. She can't help it. I've told her many times that envy breeds hatred, and she should never permit herself to hate anyone because it only ends in self-destruction. But my words fall on deaf ears. Oh yes, Tess won't like you either. Tess Linton is our housekeeper. She dotes on Fern and whoever Fern doesn't like, Tess won't like. It's a rather strange household, but an interesting one. You won't be bored, I assure you."

I smiled to myself, thinking that while I didn't wish boredom, neither did I seek a situation which might lead to conflict or further unpleasantness. I'd had enough of that.

We'd been climbing steadily for the past several minutes and now, where the road made a sharp turn, we came into a commanding view of Mystic Manor. The name suited it, for, despite its great size, there was a mysterious quality about it. The afternoon sun, reflected on the windows, made them appear to be large rectangular eyes regarding my approach and I had the uneasy feeling that the house itself was debating as to whether or not to welcome me. I tried to shrug it off, yet I could not and I felt a chill encompass me, so much so that I could feel the coldness of my clasped hands, even though they were gloved and the afternoon summer-hot.

Oh, there was beauty here. The setting was enchanting, but the manor house was not. Perhaps it was the very hugeness of the place that detracted from it. It was constructed of red brick, though the center portion——the main house, I learned afterwards——had been stuccoed over in a gray color, making it appear dull, almost ghostly. It was three stories in height, resplendent in turrets, gables, gingerbread decorations, great colonnades in front and on the coach-entrance side.

The roof was of a black slate which added no cheerful note. At a glance, I judged there were at least twenty chimneys, which gave some indication of the enormity of the house.

It stood on a bright green knoll. The grass was mowed closely and extended all the way down a sharp slope right to the edge of the river where rows of poplars had been planted as a screen for privacy from passing vessels.

Far behind the house, yet visible from where we were, stood the little building known as the Ivy Chapel. It was a private church, often talked about in the village. It was mid-afternoon and the sun's rays were beginning to slant so that some of them touched the stained-glass windows which shimmered in a dozen colors.

There were two formal gardens that I could see from our fairly lofty perch, myriad paths through arbors, and groves as well. This was a picture indicating wealth, comfort, breeding. It was an inspiring sight except for the house, which I still felt did not want me, nor any stranger, here.

"How do you like it?" Bruce asked.

"It's—awe-inspiring."

"The gardens and grounds, perhaps," he granted. "The house is drab looking and ugly. I could tell by your face that you didn't like it and I agree there's nothing attractive about that pile of bricks. I do believe, however, that you will lend some warmth and life to it. I hope so. My wish is for you to be happy here."

"Thank you, Doctor. I'd be ungrateful if I were not."

We rode down the driveway approach now and straight into the coach entrance. As the carriage pulled up, a short, gray-haired woman with small eyes and a thin-lipped mouth opened the door and came out. She was dressed in gray, with a bibbed white apron, stiffly starched, tied around her waist. She stood impassively waiting for us, showing no enthusiasm, but I knew those eyes were regarding me intently.

Bruce assisted me from the carriage, guided me up the four steps and we passed between the white colonnades.

"This is Miss Melinda Marston," Bruce told the woman in gray. "She is to live here."

"Yes, I have been so informed, Dr. Bruce."

"Melinda, this is Tess Linton, our housekeeper. If there is anything you require, ask her. Is my aunt available, Tess?"

"She is waiting in the oval room, Dr. Bruce."

"We have two drawing rooms," Bruce explained for my benefit. "The smaller one is for the family; the larger one, when my aunt entertains."

He held the door for me. Mrs. Linton had gone down the stairs and was taking my baggage from the back of the carriage. I walked into a reception hall, which was long, with an uncarpeted, highly-polished floor, some red-cushioned, high-backed chairs set against the wall and two long tables, one on either side, on which stood large lamps with stained-glass shades. Two large chandeliers were suspended from the ceiling, their lusters catching the light from the sun through the open doorway and showering the walls with jeweled colors.

For some foolish reason, such beauty excited me and

12

made me feel that the house had made the decision and was taking that way of welcoming me. It was silly, I know, yet I suppose I was grasping at straws, for, now that I was here, I felt as lonely and frightened as I had at the cemetery.

However, I had no further time to dwell on it, for Bruce was now guiding me across the main entry hall. This was two stories in height, stately and very beautiful. The staircase, halfway long this entranceway, was wide enough so that six could march abreast along it, but halfway up, it gracefully separated into two stairways. I had never seen such lovely curved banisters.

Off the entrance hall was the oval room. Its chairs were upholstered in green, with matching draperies and carpets of darker colors. The many-curtained windows which encircled the room were closed, giving it a stuffiness that made it, despite its expensive furnishings, seem unappealing.

Delphine Jager sat in one of these velvet-covered chairs, its back curving high above her head. I judged her to be about fifty. She was slender, taller than I, which made her about five feet eight. She had dark auburn hair piled on top of her head, which probably gave her some of that height. She wore an afternoon gown of fine, pale green silk, high-necked with a fringe of lace about the throat. A watch, encrusted with diamonds, was pinned to her bosom and a giant diamond ring, almost blinding in its brilliance, was on her wedding ring finger. The wedding band, I noticed later, was of yellow gold and very plain.

She was a handsome woman and must certainly have been a most-attractive girl. Her face bore no wrinkles, but she did use powder somewhat lavishly and her cheeks carried more than a trace of rouge. More of it had been employed to accentuate her lipline, but it had been done cleverly and artistically so that she looked in no way cheap.

There was a firmness and sureness about this woman, brought on, no doubt, by her wealth and station in life. I judged that she would be tolerant in forgiving mistakes, but hard as iron if she were lied to or cheated.

She arose now and extended her slim arm. "My dear, I'm glad to welcome you to Mystic Manor. Thank you, Bruce, for bringing her."

"It was a pleasure," Bruce smiled. However, my manner

was serious and decorous for I felt the occasion warranted it.

"No doubt—and I can readily see why you would think it so," Delphine said graciously. "Sit down, my dear. Bruce, don't you have a patient or two somewhere who needs your ministrations?"

"In other words," Bruce said without offense, "go somewhere else. Very well. Good afternoon, Melinda."

He bowed and left us. Delphine led me to the chair she'd occupied. She pulled over a huge hassock and lowered herself upon it gracefully. She made a lovely picture with her back to the sun, which haloed the highlights of her auburn hair.

"I'm delighted you are here, my dear child," she said. "I hope we can make your stay with us pleasant, and that you will remain for a long time."

"Thank you, Mrs. Jager. I'm most appreciative of this opportunity and very grateful for your faith in my innocence of the death of Vincent Seaton."

"Why, child, of course you're perfectly innocent. That man was here more than once. I disliked him from the start. There are—oh—a dozen women hereabouts with good reason to have shot him."

"I'm sure of it," I replied quietly. "But in the village, most people still believe I did it."

"My dear Melinda," she exclaimed, "I'm a woman of much experience with human nature. I'll tell you why you've been tried and convicted in the minds of the villagers. The women have pronounced you guilty because you're a very beautiful girl and they resent that, so they wish to make your life miserable. The men can't take your side without their women folk saying they're infatuated with you. Nobody actually believes in your guilt; they only make themselves think so. Even if Bruce hadn't proved beyond any doubt that you are innocent, I would still have been certain you were."

"I did need those words of encouragement," I admitted. "How very kind you are."

"Well, perhaps my motive is selfish." Mrs. Jager's brow furrowed. "I wanted you here because I'm rather desperate. My sister is thirty-four years old. She has known men only casually, and she's quite terrified of them. Her shyness is almost like a sickness. She has to be brought out of this shell somehow and it is my earnest hope that you will be

14

able to help her. Your work as secretary for her will be almost non-existent. My wish is for you to take Charity beyond these walls, talk to her, get her interested in something besides herself. Arrange that she meet people. Once you have penetrated her shyness, we'll give a social in her honor. If we get through that, we'll plan a larger one and then a still larger one. I want Charity to enjoy life as my sister should."

"I shall do my utmost, Mrs. Jager. It is something I have never attempted before, nor do I know if I am capable of what you ask, but it is a challenge. One I welcome, for I daresay it will take my mind off my own problem. It may be that your sister Miss Gilbert and I will be good for each other."

"You speak capably and I like your poise," Mrs. Jager said. "Only I would prefer that you address my sister by her given name. I believe she will feel much more at ease with you if you do."

'Of course. However," I held up a gloved hand, "I do not prophesy any quick results, for the overcoming of shyness must be done slowly and with care."

"You do have an understanding of it," Delphine said in a pleased voice. "We'll talk of this later. For now, I wish you to meet Charity. She's in her rooms expecting you, as a secretary and companion. You must not let her suspect you were hired for any other purpose. Tess will show you to her rooms and, later on, to your own. Please come to see me whenever you think it necessary. Should I desire your companionship, I will send for you."

I arose and found Tess standing in the doorway, waiting. Without a word, she led me to the main entrance hall, up the grand staircase where we took the left branch of it and then crossed a long upstairs hallway which eventually became a corridor off which the bedroom suites were located. All doors were closed, which gave a darkness and coldness to the hall.

Mrs. Linton's short legs moved with an amazing speed and I had to quicken my steps to keep up with her. She stopped abruptly before one door and, without knocking, turned the knob and threw the door wide. It seemed as if the gesture and the glance she cast at me as she entered the room before me seemed to say, 'Well, here you are. Now let's see what you can do.' And from the slight quirk at the corner of her mouth, it was obvious that she expected I would fail.

Though I held my temper in check, I was more than a little annoyed at the arrogance of this woman. However, I walked into the room and almost caught my breath as I gazed at the almost doll-like face of the creature who sat rigidly erect in a straight-backed chair. One hand had flown to her mouth in a gesture of fear and dismay at this abrupt invasion of her privacy. At first glance she seemed but a girl, and if Mrs. Jager hadn't told me her sister was middle-aged, I might have been fooled.

"I wish you wouldn't do that, Tess." Her voice was as soft as a child's and there was a plaintive quality to it. "You know how it frightens me when you barge in like that."

Tess gave an audible snort and began to turn away. It was more than I could bear. "One moment, Mrs. Linton."

She turned around, regarding me in utter astonishment.

"You heard what Miss Charity just said. It would frighten me also. Besides, it's a very rude thing to do. Please do not do it again. Neither to Charity nor to me."

She grew progressively redder of face as I spoke. Obviously, she had not been corrected regarding this act before and my words had so taken her by surprise, she was completely taken at a loss, for though her mouth opened, she said nothing.

"You may go now, Mrs. Linton. After Charity and I have visited, I will be pleased to have you show me to my room."

Her eyes widened in amazement as I spoke, yet I could sense a certain defiance in her manner. I knew I had the advantage at present, but I was equally aware that this woman was bound to give me trouble. I regretted it, but if I were to instill any confidence in Charity, I must, first of all, quell the arrogance this woman displayed toward her.

I detected the merest contemptuous toss of her head as she turned and left the room. After the door closed, I moved over to Charity, still seated in the chair, clutching its arms as if by doing so, she gained protection from it.

"I'm so pleased to meet you, Charity. My name is Melinda Marston."

"I know who you are. You . . . shouldn't have said that to Tess. She can be terribly mean. As mean as a—a witch."

16

"I believe it," I said with a smile and extended my hand to her in greeting. "But I'm not afraid of her."

After hesitating a moment, her hand moved out to mine, to barely touch it, then resumed its hold on the chair arm.

As I sat down, I studied her briefly. Her oval face had deep-set, dark brown eyes, but the flesh about them and on her brow had deep wrinkle lines, as if she frowned too much. However, though I could now see her fragile type of beauty was fading, it was easy to picture how beautiful she must have been not too long ago. Her skin was of a very delicate texture, her hair as fine as a baby's. She had long, slender fingers, but her arms were rather plump and so was her body. She likely overate and exercised but little. The latter, of course, I was aware of, since she kept to her suite almost entirely. As I regarded her, she shaded her eyes with her lids and her timidity so touched me that I knew I would do everything possible to enable this woman to enjoy a normal life.

"They say you killed that schoolmaster," she said, much to my surprise. Not that I hadn't heard it before. It had been whispered behind my back, even spoken aloud as I passed along the street.

"I know what they say about me," I told her. "But it is not true."

"I don't believe you killed him. I'm sure you wouldn't kill anyone. You're kind. You speak gently to me. You're not impatient with me because I'm timid. You—you don't laugh at me."

I reached over and placed my hand very lightly over hers. "My dear Charity, don't feel ashamed because you are young in heart. Don't you know that it's not only a gift, but a virtue? To be so blessed is nothing to regret. I liked you the moment I entered the room just because you are a gentle person."

Her face flooded with embarrassed color, yet I sensed her pleasure at my words. "Thank you, Miss Marston."

"Please call me Melinda, for I am already calling you Charity."

She nodded. "Melinda . . . Melinda." She said it over and over again, as if trying to get used to the sound of it and her eyes never left my face. "It's a soft name. But just because we are quiet ones—you and I—that doesn't mean we're simple-minded."

"Good gracious, no," I exclaimed. "And we shall show

17

everyone that we're two very intelligent women." I folded my hands in my lap. "Now I would like you to tell me all about yourself. That is, everything you wish to tell, so I may know you better."

"What would you like to know?" she asked, again that frightened look crossing her delicate features.

"Oh," I spoke carelessly, "if you like to arise early. What you enjoy doing through the day. If you nap and if you retire early. Just tell me anything that comes into your mind."

"I don't do very much, and I don't get up too early. I need lots of sleep because I'm not strong. I take naps too. I don't go anywhere, though.'

"Don't you like to go out?" I asked, hoping I made the idea sound exciting.

"No. I'm afraid people will laugh at me."

"In heaven's name, why?"

"I don't know. Maybe because I'm old."

"Oh, Charity," I exclaimed, giving her a chiding glance, "when I entered this room, I thought you were a young girl."

"You did?" she said and the merest excitement tinged her voice, then, as suddenly, left it. "I'm not young. I'm old now and like all old people, I go to bed early."

My head moved back and forth in negation. I could see my task would not be easy. This woman resented the fact that she was no longer young. It would be my duty to show her how wrong she was.

"Going to bed early doesn't really mean one is old. I, too, retire early many evenings."

"I go to bed because there's nothing else to do. Besides, I'm afraid to go out after dark. There are—things here—on this estate——"

"What things?" I asked.

"I don't know—things! Once I was almost choked to death. Twice my clothes were cut with a knife. They are evil things and they come only after dark."

I got up and walked to a window overlooking the south side of the estate. Things? This woman must have the mind of a small girl who was afraid of the dark. I'd have to overcome that too. I didn't know how, but perhaps Bruce could help me.

I began to turn away, but something caught my eye. I looked again. Just to the right of a rounded shrub, I saw an elongated shadow that moved as I watched, and then a figure emerged for just an instant. Because of the distance and the shrubbery, it was impossible to tell whether it was male or female, young or old, or even human. Suddenly it gave a leap into the air and with both arms flung high seemed to plunge straight into the heart of that thick bush. It looked human, yet——

I shivered inwardly, for this strange being had the ability to generate fear in me. Perhaps Charity was right after all and there were—*things*—lurking on this estate.

TWO

I resumed my chair and started to talk to Charity about myself, keeping my voice low in an effort to hold her attention. When I spoke of something that interested her, her eyes seemed to light up; then, as suddenly, she would stare straight ahead and that same frightened look I beheld upon entering would cloud her vision. I was most careful to make no mention of the murder of Vincent Seaton, nor of my subsequent arrest. Nor did she refer to it again, much to my relief. Then I began to ask her questions, easy, casual ones in the hope that I could get her started talking. Nothing that concerned herself, for she seemed to have no personal interests. Rather, I queried her concerning the family routine.

"We have dinner about seven," she replied. "Delphine dresses every night. She should because she's so beautiful. Fern does sometimes, but she's not beautiful. She only thinks she is and she is jealous of everyone who is prettier than she."

"And what about you? Don't you dress?"

"No. I'm old and ugly."

"That's nonsense, Charity. You have a lovely face, with delicate features. You remind me of a Dresden china doll."

"I do?" Her face brightened and I hoped my smile showed none of the pity I felt for this girl-woman.

"You certainly do and tonight let's surprise your sister and your niece. You will dress for dinner and I'm sure you'll look every bit as beautiful as they."

"Fern will dress tonight because of you," she said, the merest trace of excitement edging her voice. A shivery little laugh escaped her. "She's going to hate you enormously because you're beautiful and she isn't. She's just pretty."

"Oh, I hope she won't," I said, "because I want to be friends with everyone in this house."

"You can't be. Whoever Fern hates, so does Tess." Again came the laugh that was almost a sigh.

I arose. "Come—show me the dresses in your closet so that we may choose one for you to wear at dinner this evening."

"It's too late. There isn't time.

"Of course there is." I extended a hand which she reluctantly took and I drew her from the chair. "We have over an hour."

She moved slowly across the room to an open door which led into her bedroom, furnished in delicate pieces and upholstered in rose satin, with matching draperies. There were several mirrors hanging on the walls and also above the fireplace, evidence that she had not only been well aware of her one-time beauty, but extremely vain about it.

Charity, with open disinterest, opened a closet door and stepped back for me to view its interior. There was a window at the far end, curtained, but allowing light to filter through. I was amazed at the wealth of garments hanging there.

Exclaiming with delight, I went in, moved aside the dresses until I came to one which seemed to me particularly attractive. It was pale green with a series of tiny dark green bows around the neckline, to be duplicated with a double row at the hemline. Perhaps it was a little girlish for this slightly plump woman; however, I knew it was the type she would prefer. I could see that, despite what she said, she still wanted to think of herself as a young girl.

I took the pins from her hair and brushed it until it glistened. Then I center-parted it and brought it back to coil in a bun at the nape of her neck. I found two jeweled combs in one of the drawers and I slipped one on either side of the knot of hair. When she saw the change in herself, she gave a little gasp and a sigh of delight escaped her. I returned to the closet for some shoes and I believe her supply could have started a small dealer in business. I selected a pair of green velvet ones and slipped them onto her feet. Then I put a touch of rouge to her cheeks and dusted her face with powder.

"Oh, Melinda," she exclaimed, "I look—almost young."

"You do look young," I replied, eager to please this lonely woman. "And remember this always, Charity. If we are young in spirit, we need never grow old."

"I'll remember that. No matter what anyone says to me, I'll remember it. You've made me feel better, but then, that's why you did this."

I couldn't help showing my surprise. She was like a child, but with a mature intelligence and was certainly in need of some sort of help. This was more than I'd bargained for, but I was ready to meet the challenge, for Mrs. Jager had been kind to me when I needed it most. If Charity's little-girlish ways became trying, I wouldn't ever permit anyone to know it. I had a feeling she had been deeply hurt, perhaps even to the extent that she had lost not only confidence in herself, but all zest for living.

It was time now for me to change and I didn't even know where my room was. It being so close to the dinner hour, I dared not summon Mrs. Linton, so I asked Charity. She led me to the corridor and pointed to the last door along it.

"Be very pretty tonight," she said, like a child conspirator. "Let's make Fern awfully mad."

I smiled, but I didn't give her any answer. I went down the corridor to the room and opened the door. Like everyone else, I had a suite. I walked into an attractively furnished comfortable sitting room. There was a shelf of good books, magazines were on a table. There were ample lamps and candles. A settee looked most inviting, done in dark blue satin. A chandelier was suspended from the ceiling, and its lusters threw bright beams of pale color even without a light being lit, for the room was drenched with the late afternoon sunlight.

The bedroom was a pleasant corner room. It contained hooked rugs, a bed canopied in white, a large dresser, a table and three chairs. The bathroom was off it and had a sink with a slop basin beneath and an enameled bathtub on clawed legs. The bath water could be drained out through a pipe arrangement.

My bags and my small trunk awaited my attention, so I quickly unpacked. When I had everything in its proper place, I prepared myself for dinner, selecting a dress in pale lavender. It was a simple dress, as all of mine were by necessity, but it was in fashion and fit my slender figure well. I pinned to the bodice a large cameo with a tiny chain around the neck of the carved figure. The chain held a small diamond. This had been my mother's, and it was quite valuable. If I was going to please Charity—and I thought it was important that I should—then I must look my very best on this first night in Mystic Manor.

It was dark enough now that I was compelled to light several of the lamps and I had just completed this chore when someone knocked on the door. I hurried to open it and I found myself face to face with a tall, slim girl dressed in a rose gown. She had greenish-grey eyes, and dark hair which she wore high on her head. Her face was thin, with hollowed cheeks, which, nevertheless, gave her an interesting appearance. She was pretty, as Charity had said, but her eyes, as she regarded me, held a look of open impudence.

"I'm Fern Erskine," she said. "I stopped by so we could get acquainted before we met at the dinner table."

"How do you do, Miss Erskine." I realized at once that this young lady was going to be difficult, but I was determined to win her over, if possible. "I've been looking forward to making your acquaintance."

"Why?" came the blunt reply.

If I was taken aback by her rudeness, I took pains not to show it. "I suppose because I believe you're the only member of the family I haven't yet met. Also, your brother has shown me great kindness. So have both your aunts."

Her smile was mocking. "Charity doesn't amount to much. My brother suffers with all his patients. As for my aunt, it isn't in her nature to be so philanthropic."

"Perhaps you aren't aware she hired me to be a companion to her sister."

"I doubt Charity needs a companion any more than I. She keeps herself in those rooms because she wants to. As for you, I should think you would have wished to get as far away from these parts as possible after the scandal you brought upon yourself."

I found it increasingly difficult to maintain my temper in the face of this young woman's jibes.

"May I remind you, Miss Erskine," I said, speaking with quiet emphasis, "that I was not convicted of murder, nor even tried. I have done nothing wrong; therefore I see no reason why I should run away. That, in itself, would seem to point to my guilt."

"Do you intend to remain here long?"

I couldn't answer that question honestly, for I truly didn't know. But I'd not give this arrogant young woman the satisfaction of thinking she could drive me out.

"I hadn't given it a thought," I said serenely. "But I hope, for as long as Mrs. Jager deems my presence necessary."

Her critical glance flicked the length of my person, then

back to my face. "Just don't try to ingratiate yourself into my aunt Delphine's affections. I'll not tolerate it."

"There'll be no need for that. She already likes me."

"My, but you are brazen," she exclaimed. "It wouldn't surprise me if you worked on her sympathies to the extent that she included you in her will. I warn you, don't! I shan't stand for it."

"And I won't concern myself about what you will or will not stand for," I replied. "Was there anything else you wished to speak to me about? If not, I'll close the door. I still have a few things to do before I go downstairs and I find this conversation quite tiresome."

"Well, anyway," she conceded, "you're not timid. Drat it, I hoped you might be."

I closed the door on her and I thought I'd do well to heed Charity's warnings about Fern. However, I made no mention of how I felt when I returned to Charity's rooms. She was ready, though I found it necessary to touch up her hair a trifle and to adjust her dress so that it hung properly.

We entered the dining room at seven and I wondered how many had been in the family of the original owner, for the table in this room could seat thirty. Of course only a portion of it was used, but that part was beautifully set with the finest linen and silver.

Fern was already there, seated beside Bruce who promptly assisted Charity and me with our chairs. We sat across from him and his sister. Mrs. Jager would be at the head of the table as was her right.

"I presume," Bruce said, "you two ladies have met?"

"We've met," Fern said with an amused smile, "and we had quite a friendly conversation, didn't we, Miss Marston?"

I had no intention of letting her get away with that. "Of sorts, Miss Erskine."

"Oh, come now," Bruce remonstrated mildly, "both of you will be living under the same roof, seeing one another day after day. First names are in order. Don't you agree, Melinda?"

"I would prefer it," I said.

"Well," Fern said, "if you two are that friendly, by all means, first names."

I felt my face redden. It was hard to outdo Fern's barbs. The best way was to disregard them. Fortunately I was

24

spared the need for a suitable retort, or to simply face into an embarrassed silence, for just then Delphine Jager strode into the room. Apparently she waited until she'd heard everyone else go downstairs, so that she would be the last to enter. Bruce promptly sprang to his feet and went to meet her, escorted her to the head of the table and seated her.

"Good evening," she said pleasantly. "As you know, we have a new member of the household with us. Miss Melinda Marston is going to be a companion to Charity for awhile. I'm sure we shall all like her and I hope that she will like us."

This matter settled, Delphine picked up a tiny brass bell and tinkled it. The kitchen door opened; Mrs. Linton came in, leading two maids who carried heavily laden trays. Under her eagle eye, we were expertly served and as the meal progressed, I wondered how Charity didn't put on twice as much weight, and how Fern and Delphine stayed so slim. There were six courses beginning with terrapin soup, going through a fish with sauce course, an elaborate salad, beef and fowl served separately, vegetables, a floating island pudding made like none I'd ever before tasted, and finally coffee.

After dinner, she led us to the family drawing room where Fern played for half an hour on the grand piano. Its warm tones filled the room and, despite my personal dislike for the girl, she held me entranced with her skillful interpretations of Chopin and Bach. The girl was really talented and it was obvious that she enjoyed what she was doing and was completely oblivious to those around her. Truly, I was disappointed when her hands raised from the keyboard, then rested in her lap, signifying the end of the concert. We applauded politely, yet no grateful smile touched her features, making it apparent that she played only for her own pleasure.

Then Delphine arose and that was the signal the evening was concluded. As Charity and I said our good nights, Fern still sat at the piano, seemingly under the spell of the beautiful music. I could feel Bruce's eyes on me as I walked from the room and a warm flush of pleasure went through me.

We had no sooner entered Charity's sitting room and closed the door behind us than a sly smile crossed her features.

"Fern doesn't like you, does she?" she asked.

"Perhaps when she gets to know me better, she will," I replied, not wishing to get on the subject of Fern. I still felt the sting of her verbal thrusts.

"She'll never like you. She'll only hate you. She hates and hates and hates. She's always been like that. She's spoiled. My sister spoiled her."

"That's too bad," I replied, knowing it was useless to dissuade Charity from discussing the girl. "Perhaps, when she grows older, she'll change. At any rate, she'll have to. Otherwise, she'll never grow up."

"People say that about me," Charity said in a sulky voice. "But I'm not mean like Fern. I heard what she said to you before dinner. I opened my door and listened. I'm glad you talked back to her. But it will make her hate you all the more."

"Oh, Charity," I said with a sigh, for my patience was wearing thin, "let's be done with this. Suppose we talk about what we shall do tomorrow, for, as you know, I am to be your companion."

"I didn't like it at first when my sister told me you were coming here to keep me company," she said, ignoring my statement about what we would do. "But now I don't mind because I like you and you don't like Fern."

I laughed. "Oh, I'm not going to let what Fern says upset me. I fear she's the type of person who makes a habit of going around saying nasty things to people, just to make them angry."

"Do you think that's it?" Charity asked.

"I really do," I said. "And I'm not going to pay her the slightest heed. I'm interested only in you and what we shall do tomorrow."

"I don't want to do anything."

"Oh, come now," I said in a placating voice. "I noticed there are provisions for playing lawn croquet."

"I don't play. There's a tennis court, too, but I don't play that either. I'm too old."

"You're not too old and I wish you'd stop saying that." I arose, removed the combs from her hair and started to take it down. "Come into the bedroom so I can brush out your hair. And tomorrow, we're going to get some form of exercise. Nothing strenuous like tennis, understand. At least, not at first."

"Well, all right," she agreed without enthusiasm.

More and more, I had difficulty keeping in mind that this was a thirty-four-year-old woman and not a fifteen-year-old child. She pouted and sulked. She responded to praise readily and I found I could talk her into almost anything.

Then too, she could startle me. She often did, but this first night she puzzled me more than ever. She was seated before the full-length mirror in her bedroom and I was brushing her hair when I noticed a sternness creep into her features.

"Melinda, have you seen the chapel out behind the Manor House?"

"Only from a distance. I thought it very lovely."

"You are not to enter it for any reason whatsoever." Her little-girl voice was gone, and in its place was clear-cut authority. "Be sure you understand that. The chapel is used only for funerals and—weddings. No one is allowed to enter except on such occasion."

"Very well," I said. "May I ask if there is a reason for that?"

"The interior is very valuable and the rule has been set—no one goes in."

"Then I shall admire it from the outside only," I said cheerfully. "And now, if there is nothing you wish, I think I'll retire. It's been a rather exciting day for me."

"I go to bed early," Charity said. "I will never need you after I go to my rooms. I sleep like the dead and I hate to be disturbed. Good night, Melinda. I'm sure I shall come to love you very much. You are so friendly and sincere."

"Thank you, Charity. Good night then."

I left the suite, closing the door behind me. Before I had taken half a dozen steps, I heard the key turn in the lock. The act so surprised me that I paused momentarily. Then I smiled and shook my head. She was a timid soul and could feel no security unless she was behind locked doors. At the same time, it proved she was mature enough to realize she was better protected that way. Or it could be just that she desired privacy. She had told me in no uncertain terms that she did not wish to be disturbed once she had retired for the night.

I smiled and thought she needn't worry. I believed that I, too, would enjoy the privacy of my suite after a day with Charity, for I could see now that my task would be much greater than I had envisioned. Certainly the woman had no need for a secretary, since she lived the life of a recluse. But she did need to learn how to enjoy life and I hoped I would be successful in teaching her. She could be very dear and winsome when she chose and those qualities could be developed along with the maturity of which she had shown fleeting glimpses.

In my room, though my day had been full, I felt no need for sleep and decided to read in an effort to tire myself. I selected one of the books in the room, by chance *Wuthering Heights,* which I'd read before and been properly scared by. I began it again and I thought, wryly, that at least I was in the proper setting for it. At the moment, Mystic Manor seemed to me to be my own Wuthering Heights. Feeling rather foolish, I went over and locked my door, for suddenly I recalled the skulking figure of the afternoon. Perhaps that was why Charity had locked hers. She had referred to "things" prowling the estate by night.

Perhaps it was because of the personal fear I had felt when I'd been openly accused of murder, or perhaps it was because of what Charity had said, coupled with what I'd seen that afternoon, but suddenly an uneasy feeling assailed me and I could not settle myself down to the book.

I laid it on the table and walked into the still-darkened bedroom to stand before one of the windows, looking out onto the estate, faintly illuminated by a quarter moon.

So it was only by the merest chance that I saw the figure. Of course I couldn't tell if it was the same individual, but my heart gave a leap as I realized the truth of what Charity said. This time he seemed to be less apprehensive, for he came out of the shadows of the bushes and walked boldly across an open area. He was thin, merely a dark form, until he came to a stop and then deliberately turned to face the house and stare at it as if fascinated by the enormity of the structure. He also gave me a chance to make out his identity.

It was Billy Cornell, the half-witted young man who worked at the village stable in return for a daily meal and permission to bunk there at night. It was Billy without question. He wore that stocking cap which made him look foolish in summer, though he was never without it.

I had no cause to like Billy. He'd told the constable that he'd seen Vincent Seaton ride up to my cottage, dismount and walk to my door. He said it must have been

28

moments later that he'd been shot. I'd sworn I hea[ ]
sound of a gun, but Billy claimed he did, from a dista[ ]
Billy had lied, deliberately told a falsehood, but then, [ ]
was always doing that. No one believed anything he said
any more and for that I was grateful. Yet I could bear the
young man no malice, for he was not accountable for
either his words or deeds.

Billy was also a known petty thief. He would steal anything loose, not because he had need of it, but he seemed
to get a perverse pleasure in doing so. And even when
confronted with the evidence, he would always deny his
misdeeds. If he was sneaking around the estate at this
time of night, then he could very well be looking for something to steal.

I hastily threw a cloak over my shoulders, unlocked my
door and left my suite. There was a lamp burning on a
table in the hall, which helped to light my way. Downstairs,
two lamps burned on the tables in the reception hall. I
looked into the family drawing room, but found it dark.
Nor were lights burning anywhere else in the house. I
wondered if Bruce had already retired, but not knowing
the whereabouts of his suite, I decided to go outside and
chase Billy from the premises myself. I was not afraid of
him. I checked the door, noting it was unlocked, and
completely fearless, I left the house.

I walked quickly to the spot where I'd seen Billy, taking
care to move silently, but there was no longer any trace
of him. Nor did I hear any sounds to betray his presence.
However, I continued to walk along in the darkness, my
eyes seeking out any moving form. It wasn't until the
moon's path took it behind some clouds and the grounds
about me became pitch black that I began to grow frightened.

Darkness and the night had never alarmed me before,
but then, my surroundings had never been quite like this
before. Trees and bushes threw shadows—even sections of
the house created them—enormous shapes that seemed to
move as if breathing. The great house was plunged in
darkness, the lights in the hall not visible. I was tempted
to break into a panic-induced run and go back, but if I
did, I'd never again have the courage to step out of that
house again by night and since I expected this would be my
home for some time to come, I gritted my teeth and kept
on going.

had no idea where, it was just an aimless wandering in search for Billy Cornell. Suddenly I found myself staring at the little chapel. I was some distance from it still, perhaps a thousand feet, but it stood there like a great temptation. I was not supposed to enter it; therefore, I wanted to. Not tonight, however. At that moment, all I wished to do was return to the security of my rooms. I began to turn away and then I stood there, frozen in my tracks.

This was vast isolation and sounds carried. That's probably why I could hear the very faint rumble of the chapel organ. There was no question in my mind but that's what it was, and my imagination was not so active that I could be fancying the sound.

There was no melody to the notes, just random keys held down for some time, and I couldn't help believing an effort was being made not to play it so loudly that it could be heard at the house. Billy? I decided not to accost him in the chapel. Certainly he couldn't carry an organ away.

Yet for some reason, the organ notes, at this time of night when I stood alone in this dark silence, filled me with a strange and unrelenting terror. It was so great that I couldn't find the strength to flee from the spot and stood there, horror-filled, my heart pounding madly.

Nor could I take my eyes off the dark shape of the chapel. The faint moonlight was beginning to play around some of the stained-glass windows, especially toward the rear of the church. I looked skyward. The moon had vanished behind clouds. There were no longer any weird shadows along the ground, only an inky darkness, but the rear windows of the chapel seemed to be glowing slightly.

The colors began to grow more vivid though the light behind them never became very strong. Had even the moon come out from its covering of clouds, I would have given it all the credit for this phenomenon, but there was no evidence of it.

Then the light began to fade. No quickly, but as if it were being withdrawn into itself. The stained windows became dark again, the organ grew silent. The whole world was still and Stygian, and the terror with which I was already filled overwhelmed me, so much so, I regained my powers of locomotion and began to run.

I made no attempt to be silent, for my only thought was

to get away from there. My heart beat ten times
than my feet thudded against the grass, finally movin
to the gravel of a path. My mouth had gone dry; my l.
was, conversely, covered with perspiration. My lungs
ached with the heavy breathing that was a part of my
panic and when I began to grow dizzy from it all, I was
compelled to slow down.

The path along which I moved was narrow, bordered
by bushes and very dark, so that when it made one of its
turns, I usually found myself fighting the bushes until I
made out the new direction.

I heard nothing, not a semblance of a sound. Whoever
it was had moved like a wraith, but the arm that suddenly
encircled my neck was no ghostly arm, but one of flesh
and blood, strong as steel and behind it was an urge to
murder me.

My arms started up to attempt to release the strangle-
hold on my throat, but the assailant seized my left wrist
and pinned it to my side while his arm increased the
pressure, nearly strangling me. My already-tortured lungs
cried out for air and I could no longer breathe. The realization that I was about to die gave me a surge of sudden
strength. I still had a free right arm. I reached up behind
me, my fingers curved like talons. They found a face—
a human face. My nails bit deeply, dragged down and I
felt the flesh part under their sharpness.

Suddenly the arm weakened and I was released. I knew
my tearing fingernails had been close to the eyes of my
assailant, and for all I knew I'd inflicted some serious
damage upon him. Then I was flung with such force that I
fell, full length on the lawn. I grunted as the wind was
knocked out of me and though I lay there but an instant,
it seemed an eternity. I staggered to my feet and took off
on the fastest run of my life. It was impossible to tell
if I was being pursued, for my own shoes made so much
noise on the gravel they were all I could hear.

I left the path and found myself racing down the slope
of the lawn in the direction of the house and the road
leading to it. Now I did take time to look over my shoulder,
for my breath was coming in gasps. When I saw there was
no one behind me, I slowed down. My legs were trembling
so, I feared they'd no longer hold me up.

Suddenly and most unexpectedly I was faced with a new
menace. Someone was riding hard along the road and be-

31

fore I could conceal myself behind some shrubbery, the horse and rider appeared out of the gloom. To me, it seemed like the largest horse I'd ever seen and the rider was an ominous figure whose identity was masked by the night.

I turned away from the path to flee in another direction, but the grass was already slippery with early dew and my feet went out from under me. I landed in an undignified heap and while I endeavored to scramble to my feet, the horse came pounding up to me. It reared, its legs pawing the air, while I cowered, wondering if I'd escaped one danger only to run into another as bad or worse.

"Melinda!" It was Bruce's voice and none had ever seemed quite so wonderful. He dismounted quickly and helped me up. "I'm sorry I frightened you. All I saw was a figure and I thought someone was sneaking about——"

"Someone was," I said. "Doctor—I saw Billy Cornell from my window and I went out to find out what he was up to, but I couldn't locate him. I wandered about and I came upon the chapel. Someone was playing the organ and——"

"Playing the organ?" he exclaimed in tones of disbelief. "Melinda, you must be mistaken. It could have been the breeze playing tricks with your hearing."

"No . . . no, it was the organ and—and—there was a faint light behind the stained-glass windows. I could see their colors plainly. There was no moonlight at the time." I silenced any further objection he might see fit to make. "I made certain of that. There was someone in the chapel."

"At this time of night?"

"It could have been Billy Cornell. It's possible the organ fascinates him."

He nodded. "Yes . . . it could have been. He's addled enough to do a thing like that. Come on, we'll go see."

He vaulted into the saddle, reached down and before I could offer the slightest objection, he swung me up before him and the horse moved off at a trot. His strong arm around my waist was most comforting.

I said anxiously, "I was told not to go into the chapel under any circumstances."

"Bosh," he said promptly. "Who told you that?"

"Charity—and she meant it."

"Oh, Charity," he said tolerantly. "She's taken it upon herself to regard that chapel as her own. It's not. She has

32

no right to deny you or anyone admission. Anyway, place is kept locked, but if Billy got in, maybe we can to

I shuddered when we came into view of the chapel a I felt his arm tighten about me as if for assurance. Then we were there and he dismounted, lifted me down gently and we walked to the double-doored entrance. We paused to listen, but there was only silence. He tried the latch. They doors were locked. He shook them impatiently, but they remained locked.

I said, "Never mind, Doctor. Perhaps I was mistaken."

"I know you were," he said, with a smile. "Nobody ever goes in there unless one of us dies. Look up at the little steeple. Can you see the bell? The villagers say it only rings when there's grave trouble. That's nonsense. It never rings—because we don't ring it. Shall we go back home now?"

"I may have imagined the organ music and the light, but not the attack made upon me," I said, disregarding his offer to take me back.

"Attack? When? What sort of attack?"

"Just before you arrived. I was running from the chapel along the path. Someone stepped out behind me and tried to throttle me with his arm. I say *his* because I feel quite sure it was a man, though I have no proof."

"Did he hurt you?"

"He meant to kill me. I could tell. But I had one hand free and I managed to scratch and gouge him. Around the eyes, I think. It forced him to let go of me and I ran. Then you came and frightened me all over again."

"Forgive me, Melinda. Let me take you back to the Manor."

He lifted me onto the animal, hoisted himself into the saddle and the horse went pounding down to the house. He unsaddled the animal, threw the saddle and blanket over a hitch rack and let the horse go.

"He'll head for the stable. He knows the way," he explained.

We went inside and Bruce took me straight into the family drawing room where he lit a lamp. He made me sit down while he held the lamp and bent over me. His fingers touched my throat gently. They were the cool, professional fingers of a physician.

"There are signs of bruises. . . . Let me see your right hand. Ah. You *are* hurt."

"No," I said, "not at all."

"There's blood—your fingers——"

I looked at them. It was true. Dried blood coated the nails. Bruce disappeared for a few seconds and returned with a cloth soaked in water. He cleaned off the blood. My hands were neither cut nor bruised.

"You're right—it's not your blood. Whoever waylaid you, Melinda, will carry the scars for a time. Now who in the world would do this? Billy Cornell, suddenly angered enough to attack you because you saw him prowling? I know him to be a liar and, sadly, more than a nuisance, but never have I known of him to inflict physical violence upon anyone before."

"I don't know who attacked me. But I believe that tonight I was meant to die," I said.

Doctor Bruce looked properly thoughtful. "You may not believe this, Melinda, but never before in this modern day has physical violence been committed on this property."

"I believe it, Doctor," I replied. "And I hesitate to point the finger of suspicion at anyone. I know how horrible it is to be accused of a crime one hasn't committed."

He sat down opposite me. "Poor Billy isn't accountable for his behavior. I feel badly for having had to lash him with the whip today, but the horses could have panicked and injured not only him, but also you, by throwing you from the carriage."

And you too, I thought. "Do you suppose he is angry because his testimony at the hearing wasn't believed?"

"It's possible," Bruce conceded. "He could also have been angry with me because of what I did to him this afternoon, and taken it out on you. I shall certainly question him about it, but he'll deny it—if it was he."

"Oh, please don't," I exclaimed. "Let the matter drop. It probably was he, but if he is accused, he will only brood on it the more and I may have further trouble with him."

"If that is the way you want it. I'm only sorry I wasn't here."

"I thought of summoning you and looked for you downstairs. I didn't know where your suite was."

"Let's go upstairs now and I'll show it to you. Should anything like that happen again, summon me. I only hope I won't be out on a sick call."

"Of course," I said, with sudden realization. "I had forgotten a doctor's time is never his own."

"Oh, I wasn't on a call," he replied. "I was out riding. I do it often at night. I find it relaxes me. Also it helps me to think about my patients and how best to help them."

"You're a very dear man, Dr. Bruce," I said impulsively.

"Thank you, Melinda," he said, his features serious. "But when you address me, will you leave off the *doctor*? I think a great deal of you too, you know, and I don't want anything to happen to you. I daresay that after tonight, you will wish to leave the Manor."

"Had I somewhere to go, I would," I replied in all honesty. "But you forget that I am greatly beholden to your aunt. I have but a few dollars to my name."

Bruce paused at the foot of the stairs to regard me thoughtfully. "I don't blame you for not wanting to remain here and if you will allow me, I would like to make you a loan sufficient to sustain you until you find a teaching position elsewhere."

"I wouldn't think of it," I replied. "But I thank you for the gesture. I shall remain here, for I doubt, with the cloud of suspicion of murder hanging over my head, I would be able to find a suitable position anywhere."

"It is indeed a trying situation for you," he said. "However, I will confess that I am pleased you will be with us for awhile longer, at least. I'm of the firm opinion you can help Charity, who seems to get no pleasure out of life and lives in a dreamlike world of her own. Also, I'm hopeful that some of your innate goodness will rub off on my sister. I apologize for her rudeness tonight at the table."

"I'm sorry she took such an instant dislike to me."

"Oh, it isn't just you. Fern makes a habit of rudeness. It seems to make her feel superior. However, you stood up to her and I liked that. She respects you and, in time, may even emulate you."

I didn't voice my doubts, merely smiled, and said, "I shall do my best not to let her attitude irritate me."

"For that, I express my deepest thanks, and also my relief, for I firmly believe we need you here."

Despite what I'd been through, I felt my cares wash away, as if by magic, at his words. I was fortunate indeed, to be a paid companion in this house and to be accepted so warmly by all here except Fern. Of course, I wasn't really acquainted with Mrs. Jager, but I hoped we would become firm friends.

Bruce escorted me upstairs and before he accompanied me to my door, he pointed out his suite. It was in a further corridor and at the very end. Feeling reassured, I bade him good night, closed the door of my room and, after a moment's hesitation, locked it.

THREE

The next morning I slept later than usual, due, no doubt, to my harrowing experience of the night before. I bathed and dressed hastily, then left my suite, going directly to Charity's. I knocked on her door and, much to my surprise—for she'd told me the day before that she usually slept late—she was dressed and ready to join me.

She informed me that I need feel no qualms about rising late, for breakfast was served whenever a member of the family came downstairs and desired it. I felt relieved to hear it. Like the evening meal, this was also lavish—with fruit, cereal, eggs, ham, hot muffins and much yellow butter and rich cream for the coffee and cereal.

Charity maintained a demure silence through the first part of the breakfast, giving her entire attention to the food. It was obvious that there was nothing wrong with her appetite, for she was on her fourth muffin and second helping of everything on the table.

When I was certain she'd had sufficient nourishment so that her appetite would not be spoiled by what I was about to say, I related what had happened to me last night.

"How horrible," she exclaimed when I finished my story. Her childlike features were drawn in lines of concern.

"Fortunately, I was able to escape whoever attacked me, but I believe he meant to kill me."

"Do you know who it was?"

"I didn't see his face, but I scratched it so he won't be difficult to identify. I did recognize the person who was skulking about the estate as Billy Cornell."

"I never knew of Billy to hurt anyone."

"Nor I," I admitted.

"Were you hurt?"

"It was painful and I have bruises about my neck. That's the reason for the dress I'm wearing. The collar conceals them."

"Oh, Melinda," Charity's voice quavered and I thought her to be on the verge of tears, "please don't leave me. Please don't leave the Manor. I like you so much and I want you with me and I know that, with you around, I won't be afraid of people. In fact, I might even get to like them."

"I'm not leaving," I assured her. "But I am sorely puzzled about that organ playing in the chapel, especially when you told me no one was allowed in there."

"No one is."

"Bruce told me otherwise."

She set down the roll she was buttering and her eyes beseeched me. "All right, I told a fib, but I meant no harm. It was just that I thought you might be frightened by it. You see, the chapel has a reputation for being haunted. Of course it isn't true, but the villagers believe it and because of that, we have a difficult time getting servants to come here to work—just because of that crazy superstition. At one time, the legends grew so bad that the villagers kept coming out here to view it. That's when Delphine finally decided to lock it up and allow no one in. Since then, the ghost stories have died away and we have peace here once again."

"Don't you believe I heard the organ played?"

"I don't want to believe it or I might become scared. Did you go to see if someone was in there?"

"Yes. Bruce and I went there, but the door was locked."

Her face brightened. "There, you see? You imagined it. You got frightened and imagined it. No one ever goes there, Melinda. The organ hasn't been played in years. It's just that you knew there must be an organ in the chapel and you thought you heard it. Sometimes I listen to the wind in the trees and it sounds like music—maybe like an organ."

"Charity," I insisted, "there was also light through the windows."

She passed that off too with her childlike simplicity of thought. "Even the stars can make the stained glass shine sometimes. I guess now you can see why we don't let anybody in the chapel. If you'd been from the village, you'd have run home and told everyone there was a ghost in there."

"I didn't imagine the attack on me," I said, but I was ready to give the whole thing up. Charity would believe only what she wished and have a ready explanation for anything else.

"Oh, I guess that happened all right. I told you there were *things* here. . . . Maybe Billy is to blame for it all. But it wasn't any ghost that hurt you. And we were talking about ghosts. Did you know that in the village it's said when the chapel bell rings somebody always dies?"

"I don't understand why they're afraid of a chapel bell," I said.

Charity looked very smug and very wise. I supposed it wasn't often that she was able to tell anyone anything, so she was feeling quite superior at the moment.

"It's supposed to be cursed because it came off a slave ship. One of those awful ships—you know—I don't pay much attention, but all this scares the servants. We can't even get any to sleep in."

"I promise I won't talk about it. I don't like to admit I was frightened anyway."

Charity stirred four spoonfuls of sugar into her heavily-creamed coffee. "Would you like to see the inside of the chapel?"

"Why—yes—but I don't want to put you to any trouble."

"I'll get the key from Delphine soon as we finish breakfast. I haven't been inside since Uncle Thaddeus died. I forget how long ago that was." She gave me a sunny smile. "I don't even remember Uncle Thaddeus very much."

As soon as we finished, Charity hurried upstairs while I waited near the door. Moments later she came down again, waving a large brass key triumphantly over her head.

It was a pleasant walk to the chapel, for the day was sunny, with a cloudless blue sky overhead. A faint breeze wafted the perfume of the gardens to us and the beauty of the grounds made the setting seem like a fairyland. Gone was the fear I was so beset with last night and I looked about, trying to locate the exact spot where I'd been attacked, but there were so many paths and the lawns so extensive, it was impossible to pick it out.

We were now close to the chapel and it looked as pretty and attractive by day as it had seemed forbidding by night. It was partially covered with ivy, trimmed back so none of it obscured the windows. In the white steeple I could see the large brass bell. It seemed far too huge for this little private church.

"Why did they ever install such a great bell?" I asked Charity.

"I told you—it came off a slave ship."

"Yes, you did tell me, but I still don't see why they added it to this chapel."

"I don't know about that, Melinda."

We walked up to the double doors and Charity inserted the key, turned it and the lock opened easily. Charity stepped back.

"You go first," she offered. "This place has always scared me. Every time I see it, I think of all the people who died and were taken here. I couldn't bear going in if I were alone."

I pushed open one of the doors. The hinges were creaky and resisted, proving the door hadn't been often opened. The chapel was already well-illuminated by the sunlight streaming through its several windows, so that it actually looked inviting and pleasant.

There was a wide center aisle and two end aisles. There were about fifteen rows of pews, all of hard wood and beautifully carved. There was a lectern in place of a pulpit and the altar seemed to be of normal size to me.

Above my head was a low ceiling, actually the floor of the organ loft, as I learned later. I walked down the aisle slowly, looking with admiration at the stained-glass windows, for each was a work of art. Near the front of the chapel I turned around. Charity still stood near the door, making no attempt to enter any further than that. I looked up at the loft where the organ was located. It was a medium-sized instrument, its pipes gilded, and two tall candles were placed on either side of the keyboard to give maximum light by night or, perhaps, on a dull and rainy day.

It was a charming place—quaint and most interesting —especially since it was supposed to have been closed up for seven years, yet there was very little dust. I wondered who came in to clean it. Probably Mrs. Linton. She didn't look the type to be frightened by ghosts. I walked back to rejoin Charity.

"You see," she said, "not a sign of a ghost or a midnight organ player."

"It's a lovely place," I said. "I've never before seen anything like it. It seems such a waste that it's used only for funerals."

"And weddings," Charity said with a smile. "No need to worry about that though. Nobody in this house is going to get married in a hurry. Not that one of us wouldn't like to—and I don't mean me or Delphine or Bruce and I especially don't mean Tess Linton, the housekeeper."

"That leaves Fern," I said. "Is she engaged?"

"No, though she certainly expected to be. But she got fooled. She's supposed to be nursing a broken heart, but she's too mean to mourn anyone."

"You mean, the man she was in love with died?" I asked, feeling proper sympathy for Fern and, perhaps, a better understanding of her behavior toward me.

"He was murdered," Charity said.

"Surely you don't mean Vincent Seaton," I exclaimed.

"I do. She was seeing an awful lot of him. She loved him, but he didn't love her. She couldn't hold him any more than any other woman could, I guess."

My smile was thoughtful as I realized that Charity had the wisdom of a mature woman when she recognized Vincent for what he'd been. My sympathies were even greater for Fern, for I could realize the shock she must have received when she realized he was merely a philanderer.

"I'm sorry to hear that. I can understand how she felt."

"Did he throw you over too?"

"No," I told her. "When I discovered what a shallow person he was, I refused to see him."

"He really loved you though," Charity stated firmly.

"Nonsense," I scoffed. "Vincent loved no one but himself."

"No," she contradicted. "I heard him tell Fern he loved you and hoped one day, when he was ready to settle down, to marry you."

I must have looked my surprise for Charity, with greater emphasis in her voice, went on. "Yes, he did. Whether you believe it or not, he said that. Now are you sorry you stopped seeing him?"

"No," I replied, "though I'm sorry for what happened to him."

"Did you really love him?" she persisted.

"I thought I did," I replied. "But perhaps it was just an infatuation. I was flattered that he showed me attention. I was lonely. He could be very gracious and charming and, yes—kind."

"He wasn't generous though. He never took Fern any-where."

41

"Perhaps she didn't wish to go."

She shrugged. "Maybe. They used to walk around the estate or go down and sit by the river. I guess she didn't care about going anywhere. She just wanted to be with him. Now you know why she hates you. She even said you killed him."

"Oh, she didn't," I exclaimed in disbelief.

"Yes, she did, but Bruce could have done it. Maybe he was the one who killed Vincent."

"Oh, Charity, do think of what you are saying."

"I mean it. He didn't want Fern to see Vincent. He didn't want Vincent around here because Bruce knew what Vincent was. One day I saw Vincent on the grounds and I knew Bruce was home and painting and would probably see him from his studio window so I went out on the grounds and hid. Sure enough, soon Bruce came out and he and Vincent started to quarrel."

"Oh, Charity, you shouldn't be telling me all this."

"I've got to. You should know about it so you'll understand why Fern hates you. Anyway, Bruce ordered him off the grounds and Vincent refused to leave. Then Bruce told Vincent if he did anything to hurt Fern, Bruce would kill him. That's just what he said—'I'll kill you.'"

All this information came as a shock to me and I dared not dwell on it. I had no idea there had been ill-feeling between Bruce and Vincent; nor did I know that Fern had been in love with Vincent. Nevertheless, I felt my loyalty belonged to this family. They, of everyone in the village, were the only ones who had come to my aid with the exception, of course, of Attorney Cecil Todd. Therefore, I felt it necessary to warn Charity to remain quiet about what she had told me.

"Oh, no one at Mystic Manor gossips to an outsider," she explained, as if that settled everything. "I only told you because you're one of us now. I like you very much, Melinda. I hope you'll stay."

"Thank you, Charity. I will."

I was bestowing no favor on her for I had nowhere else to go. My money amounted to precious few dollars. I'd been so proud to have secured this position of teaching at the village and I'd determined to make good at my profession. Instead, I'd ended up being accused of murder though, for lack of evidence, I'd never been tried for it. However, the shame of suspicion still hung over my head.

And yet, I hadn't heard the worst, for Charity exploded still another bomb in my face.

"Do you know who I think killed Vincent?" Her little-girl voice was almost a whisper.

I wanted to get off the topic of Vincent and murder, but I knew Charity by now and it would be useless to change the subject until she had tired of it.

"I haven't the faintest suspicion," I replied patiently.

"Fern did it." She was engaged in the act of locking up the chapel and she didn't look at me.

"Charity—you can't mean it!" I exclaimed.

"Oh, don't look so shocked. She could kill a man easily enough, and she knows how to use a gun. What's more, she has one. A revolver that she keeps hidden in her rooms. I know something else too."

"Perhaps you'd best not tell it to me," I said. "Remember, I've been accused of this murder and most of the villagers still believe I did it. I might take advantage of anything you tell me."

Her eyes reproached me. "I'd deny I ever told you anything. They'd believe me."

"Oh, Charity," I cried out and my voice was a plea, "why must you persist in talking of a subject which is most painful to me?"

"Then you did love him. You did!" she exclaimed.

"No! But I have suffered so much and you're bringing all the pain back—all the humiliation and misery I endured from the moment Vincent was found dead on my porch until your nephew led me away from the grave."

"But, Melinda, you're my friend. That's why I'm telling you."

Those childlike eyes filled with tears. Compassion swept over me as I realized that, in her way, Charity believed she was doing me a favor.

"I'm sorry, my dear," I said quietly. "I didn't wish to hurt you. I realize though we've known one another briefly, we're friends." Then, so as to further assure her of it, I added, "Have you anything further to tell me?"

Her head moved slowly up and down. "Vincent Seaton was here, on this estate, the night he was killed. I know. I saw him."

I wondered how much more I could endure. But now, I'd heard so much, I wanted to know how much more

Charity could or would reveal. Everything, I imagined, and I dared not think of what it might be.

"Tell me about it." I wondered if, now that she realized I was truly curious, she would hold back information.

Her eyes brightened, for she was eager to tell her tale. "He was visiting Fern, of course. He was riding that big gray of his—the one they discovered near your cottage after they found Vincent dead. I think he came to tell Fern he wouldn't see her again and they quarreled."

"Does Bruce or your sister know of this?" I asked.

"Nobody knows. Delphine would laugh at me and Bruce wouldn't believe Fern would kill Vincent."

"Do you realize what you're saying?" I exclaimed. "Did you see her do it?"

"Of course I didn't see her. But I'll bet she shot Vincent and got him on his horse. He was still alive and he went back to your house because you were the one person he loved."

"Oh, Charity," I said, my voice a bare whisper, for I was shocked at the picture she had just painted for me.

"You won't tell them what I said, will you?" she asked plaintively. "We're friends, remember."

"I won't tell them," I replied with a sigh. "For you don't have enough facts to prove your case."

"But you will beware of Fern? I'm afraid she might harm you——"

"I'll be on guard," I assured Charity, who, now that she had unburdened herself of her secrets, seemed frightened. I felt a little ill myself and decided that now was the time to turn her mind to subjects of a wholesome and pleasant nature.

I suggested we inspect the tennis court. Charity guided me to it, but displayed no enthusiasm as I talked of the game, so we proceeded to one of the formal gardens where I was able to forget the unpleasantness of the last few moments as my eyes feasted on the beauty of the blossoms blooming before me. I praised the roses and the beds of pinks and ragged-ladies.

"How many gardeners are employed here?" I asked, mostly to change the subject.

"Seven—they don't live here though. Go home every afternoon. Nobody wants to live here. They're all scared."

"I must admit, Charity, that I'm not too easy in mind myself after what happened last night. I would suggest that you not venture out after dark unless someone is with you."

"I don't like the nighttime," she said promptly. "I go to bed early. I guess when it comes down to it, I'm afraid to go out on the estate after dark too."

"It's wise to be cautious. Now, what shall we do the rest of the day? Do you have any letters you wish written?"

She smiled shyly, the little girl again. "Yes, Melinda. I have some letters I wish you would write for me. I'll sign them though."

"Very well. That's what I'm here for. Perhaps we can have one of the servants post them in the village when they go home this afternoon."

"I don't think so," she said in a sing-song voice, taunting me pleasantly.

"What do you mean? Of course they'll post your letters."

"You won't have them done. There are—almost two hundred."

I came to a quick stop. "Charity, what are you talking about?"

"A surprise." Her laugh was one of pleasure. "Delphine is going to give a big dinner dance in my honor and we're going to invite two hundred couples. You have to write the invitations."

"A party for you," I exclaimed. "How nice! Two hundred couples! That means four hundred people."

"Oh, they won't all come. We invite some of them just out of courtesy. Last year about a hundred and twenty came. We did have a lovely time. Or they did. I didn't enjoy myself. But I will this year because you're here."

"You'd enjoy it anyway. With the music and dancing——"

"Oh, I don't know how to dance. I don't even like to, and if any of the younger men ask me to dance, it's only because they feel sorry for me. I hate being felt sorry for. Nobody has to feel sorry for me. I've got everything I want and more."

Her manner was a mixture of shyness and defiance and it sorely puzzled me. But then, since I was here for the sole purpose of being her companion, I would have a lot of time to study her, learn her moods, help her to acquire confidence.

"Of course you have," I said. "You're a very lucky——"

I almost said "woman" and changed it to "girl" at the last instant. She smiled and nodded and I knew I'd done it properly. She did regard herself as a girl—even at the age of thirty-four.

We went to her rooms where she handed me a list of the guests. It was a formidable one and when I saw that the dinner was to be held in less than two weeks, I sat down immediately, for I knew there was scant time for me to write and dispatch the invitations and allow the recipients to mail back their acceptances or regrets. Then, too, there was the affair to be planned and I'd had no experience in that sort of thing. I did hope Mrs. Jager would lend a hand or at least make a few suggestions. I knew I could expect little help from Mrs. Linton. Her loyalties were with Fern and the latter despised me.

As my thoughts dwelt on her, the horror of what Charity had revealed to me that morning came flowing back into my mind. Could Fern have murdered Vincent? Or could Bruce be guilty? Was that why I'd been invited to live here? As a solace to their conscience? Or perhaps so they could watch me? I couldn't believe it. I wouldn't believe it. Charity was only guessing and had planted ugly suspicions in my mind. If I were to believe them, I'd be as cruel as the villagers had been to me.

I shrugged off the depressing thought and concentrated on the letters. Charity went down for her noonday meal, but I was uninterested in food because of the late breakfast. Also, I was most anxious to begin work on the letters. I was a little surprised that Mrs. Jager had seen fit to have a dinner-dance so soon after my arrival and the thought occurred to me that it might not be a very happy evening so far as I was concerned. I was a social outcast since the death of Vincent Seaton.

When Charity returned to her rooms, she excused herself and went into her bedroom to nap. She was there most of the afternoon and when she arose, I set her to work signing the invitations I had written. This kept her busy until it was time to dress for dinner. I offered to assist her, but she declined and I left the suite.

I was anxious to see Bruce for I'd heard his voice outside the door while I was writing and I was eager to learn if he'd seen Billy Cornell. However, I was unable to locate him downstairs in the family drawing room. I entered a larger one, done in gold, and its magnificence fairly took my breath away. I crossed the hall to a room on the opposite side and knew it must be a banquet hall. I understood now why Mrs. Jager could invite such a huge number of guests.

The room was very long, running almost the length of the main house. An enormous table set in the center of the room seemed to be far smaller than it was, for it was surrounded by a great deal of space. No doubt there were other tables and many chairs stored away.

I stepped from the room and was confronted with Mrs. Linton. She stood, her hands resting on her hips, her eyes regarding me with ill-concealed hatred.

"I'm looking for Dr. Bruce," I said. "Can you tell me of his whereabouts?"

"That's what I'm here for," she said. "But it ain't easy for me to find one who's gallivanting around, snooping in every nook and corner of the house."

"Mrs. Linton, although I'm a paid companion in this house, I also consider myself, to some extent, a guest. I intend to treat you with courtesy, but I expect the same treatment in return. Now will you tell me, please, where I may find Dr. Bruce?"

"He's in his studio, painting."

"I have no knowledge of its location." I wondered if I was going to have to get down on my knees to this woman whenever I had a request.

"The third floor," she said. "Find it yourself."

"Thank you," I said, and turned away from her, telling myself she wasn't worth getting angry over. I marched up the stairs and automatically took the right fork as everyone else seemed to do. I went down the corridor searching for the stairway to the top floor and I found it at the end of the hall.

These stairs were narrower, very steep and led to a hallway so eternally dark it was always illuminated by candlelight. Every door was tightly shut save the one at the end, where afternoon sunlight streamed in and even spilled out into the hall. I began to walk faster, and as I neared the room I knew this was Bruce's studio, for I could smell the turpentine and paints.

He stood before an easel, palette and brush in hand, while he worked painstakingly on an oil of Charity. Before I could examine the portrait to any extent, he heard my approach and turned to greet me. He put down the brush and palette and extended his hands toward me.

"Melinda, I'm delighted to see you. I left word with Tess——"

"Yes, she informed me. May I look at your painting, Bruce?"

"Of course. Do you recognize it?"

It was a head-and-shoulders painting of Charity, a rather large one and greatly detailed. It was evident that Bruce was a highly talented artist, for he had captured that shy-girl look in a woman of thirty-four and actually made it believable. You knew his subject was mature in years, but you sensed she still clung to her youth.

"What a splendid likeness," I said. "You're certainly not an amateur, but rather an extremely capable artist."

"Thank you, Melinda. And now, may I ask if you have fully recovered from your frightening experience of last night?"

"Quite," I replied. "I'm reminded of it only when I touch my neck. There are a few sensitive spots."

"And bruises," he replied, looking grim.

"That's really why I wished to see you," I said. "I didn't wish to disturb you from your work."

"I'm always happy to see you," he replied. "You're refreshing to be around. Besides, have you forgotten I sent for you?"

"Thank you, sir. And now if I may, I'd like to ask you if you saw Billy Cornell today. I'm most anxious to know if his face was marked from my nails."

"I'm sorry, Melinda. I inquired at the stable. They believed he slept there last night, but he was not in sight when they opened for business, nor had he put in an appearance when I left town this afternoon."

"Was this unusual on his part?"

"They indicated it was, so I'm inclined to believe, as you do, that it was he who attacked you. Naturally, if his face is scratched, he'll stay out of everyone's way. He's not so stupid as to reveal himself. However, there aren't many places he can hide and I understand the village people no longer regard him as quite the harmless soul they thought him formerly. I believe if they learn of his whereabouts, I will hear of it."

He led me over to a large, high-backed chair, apparently

used in posing his subjects. It was well padded and I sat down gratefully, for, though I'd done little this day, I felt strangely fatigued.

"I wonder," I said musingly, "if he could know anything about the murder of Vincent."

"I don't know, but if we could find him, I'd certainly question him about it."

"I'm thinking that's why he attacked me. I'm sorely puzzled by his action. It just doesn't make sense to me."

"Nor me. And I believe you have a point there. Of course, we know he lied when he gave evidence. It could be that he resented the fact that he wasn't believed. It's a well-known fact that Vincent used to give him little knick-knacks."

"I know. He was fond of Vincent."

I was silent a moment and Bruce, sensing I was troubled, asked, "Is something else bothering you?"

I nodded. "Mrs. Jager is giving an affair for your Aunt Charity. I'm wondering just how I will be accepted."

"You're accepted by this family. I imagine the guests will keep that in mind."

"I hope you're right."

"Don't worry about it," Bruce said. "I'll be there."

"And I'll be grateful for your company."

He laughed. "Melinda, I mentioned wanting to paint your portrait the day I brought you here. I'm serious. Will you pose for me?"

"I'm honored, sir," I said, feeling a warm glow of pleasure.

"I'm the one to be honored. And Melinda, try not to brood too much on what happened to Vincent. You're innocent. In time, the villagers will come to accept that."

"No. They never will believe in my innocence until the murderer has been found. I only wish I knew how to go about finding out who did it."

"My dear, you're not a detective," he said, trying to reason with me. "Take comfort in the fact that Aunt Delphine is pleased to have you with us and Charity—well, I could tell last night how she regards you. She was actually happy at the table. Usually, she is morose and often she even refuses to come downstairs to dine with us. That, I might add, upsets Aunt Delphine very much. She is a martinet when it comes to the evening meal."

I arose. "Then I must leave, for there is little time to dress."

"Oh," he gripped my arm lightly as we walked to the door, "try not to let Fern annoy you too much. You see, she was in love with Vincent and blames you for the fact that he lost interest in her."

"But that isn't so."

"Perhaps not," Bruce said, and I wondered if he sounded convinced. "Nevertheless, she believes it firmly. Also, I feel I must tell you that she is of the opinion you shot Vincent."

"In that conviction, she is not alone," I said with a sigh.

"I know you're innocent," he said.

"How can you be so certain?" I asked, then felt myself coloring, for I knew why I'd asked the question. How could he be so certain unless he himself was guilty? I was ashamed of the thought, yet I knew now it was implanted in my mind, and it would fester there until I knew who had killed Vincent.

At the door, I turned to go, but Bruce held me back a moment. "Charity takes a long nap every afternoon. I've tried to break her of the habit, but it can't be done, so let her enjoy herself. Will you take that time to pose for me? It gives us the remainder of the afternoon. You see, my office hours are only until two, so I'm home early unless there are emergencies."

"Tomorrow at three then," I said. "I consider it a great privilege."

I hurried away, knowing I didn't have much time, for I had to change and then help Charity. I hastily washed, put on another dress, rearranged my hair and added a touch of rouge to my lips. A quick glance in the mirror indicated I was presentable so I hurried to Charity's suite and knocked on the door. There was no answer and while that puzzled me I wasn't alarmed.

I went downstairs alone and discovered I was the first to appear but the others soon arrived, including Charity, who offered no explanation of why she hadn't answered my knock. Mrs. Jager came last, as usual, and the procedure was exactly the same as before. The conversation was interesting and spritely enough and, thank heavens, didn't touch upon either murder nor ghosts.

No one seemed to resent Delphine's queenly attitude,

for she was never overbearing. I was sure that none in this household even gave it a thought. I wouldn't either if I remained here long enough.

FOUR

We were finishing dessert and coffee when Mrs. Linton stormed into the room, holding an object in one hand. She placed it directly before Mrs. Jager.

"There," she said triumphantly, "I guess that answers a lot of questions."

"What is it?" Mrs. Jager asked.

We were all looking at the leather purse Mrs. Linton had brought. It was a rather large one, of the clasp variety, in which a man would be apt to carry his money and perhaps a few small personal papers.

"That," Mrs. Linton said dramatically, "belonged to Vincent Seaton and I found it"—she pointed a finger straight at me—"in her room."

"It's not true," I said promptly, "for I never had anything belonging to Vincent Seaton."

"I found it in one of your carpetbags, that's where it was. Didn't get there by itself."

"Do you make a habit of going through the baggage of guests?" I asked angrily.

"Guest indeed. Far's I'm concerned, you're a dangerous person to have under the same roof."

"Just a minute," Mrs. Jager interrupted sternly. She was directing her oncoming anger at Mrs. Linton, not me. "I know of your snooping habits, Tess, but this is going too far."

"I wouldn't have looked if it wasn't for your own good, Mrs. Jager. That's all I had in mind. She's a murderess——"

"That will do," Mrs. Jager said sharply.

"It was in her bag. First one I looked in—I was putting them away——"

"They were already put away," I said.

"Well, it makes for an interesting evening," Fern commented cynically.

"A disgusting one," Bruce broke in. "Miss Marston should not be subjected to anything so humiliating."

"I agree," Mrs. Jager said. "However, if it is the property of the late Vincent Seaton, we'd best know about it."

"It is," Mrs. Linton exclaimed. "Anyone can see from the papers that it is. And don't deny it wasn't there, young lady."

"I do deny it," I replied, my defiance matching hers.

Mrs. Jager opened the purse. It contained some silver and copper coins and a slender, folded packet of paper currency. There were also several documents which she read.

"This is undoubtedly Vincent Seaton's property," Mrs. Jager said with a sigh. "Melinda, we are all interested in hearing what you have to say about this."

"Now just a minute." Bruce threw his napkin on the table and arose. "I think this has gone far enough. Melinda happens to be a guest in this house and should be treated as such. So far as the purse is concerned, it could have been placed there by anyone—even Mrs. Linton."

An explosive breath escaped Mrs. Linton's lungs. "Dr. Bruce, to think that you would say that to me when all I'm trying to do is keep the people under this roof safe."

"Mrs. Jager," I said, "I'd like to ask your housekeeper just why she did such a thing."

"I told you," Mrs. Linton said boldly. "I don't like living in the same house with a murderess."

"Tess," Mrs. Jager said, "are you sure you found the purse among Melinda's things?"

"You think I'd lie?" Mrs. Linton asked indignantly.

"I have no idea how this purse got into this house, but I do know you have shown an intense dislike for Melinda since she came here. Therefore, I'm of the opinion you might be tempted to make trouble for her."

"I'll give my notice now," Mrs. Linton said promptly.

"Oh, stop it," Mrs. Jager said tartly. "You won't leave nor will I dismiss you, and you know it. But you are not to touch anything in Miss Marston's rooms from now on."

"Don't worry, I won't," she retorted. "A fine lot of thanks I get for trying to protect those I love."

Bruce burst into laughter and so did Mrs. Jager. However, I was too consumed by misery to see the humor in any of this.

"Mrs. Jager," I said, "the purse should be taken to the constable and turned over to him with the story of how it was discovered. I cannot believe it was in my baggage, but if it was, someone put it there. It follows, if such is the case, that person knows something about the murder of Mr. Seaton."

"You are not afraid that the finding of the wallet among your possessions will incriminate you, Melinda?" Mrs. Jager asked.

"I am afraid of nothing that concerns the murder, for I'm totally innocent of it."

"Then you and I, Melinda, will go to the constable tomorrow. Before we go, Tess, it would be well for you to think about this and if you wish to correct any errors in your story, the place to do it is before us, not before the constable."

"I told you what I found. That's all there is to it, but every word is the truth," Mrs. Linton said angrily. "If you want to take the part of this—this—woman, that's your right, but you can't make me believe she's the innocent little dove she pretends to be."

"That will do," Mrs. Jager said calmly. "We shall not discuss this again."

"Why not?" Fern asked. "I think it should be discussed. I never approved of you taking Melinda Marston into this house. I believe Tess."

Charity, who had so far remained shyly silent, raised her head. "It's all just too horrible to think that Melinda could kill anyone. Delphine, I wish you would stop Fern from talking about it. It's spoiled my appetite and ruined my digestion."

Fern, in anger, pushed her chair back and rushed from the room. Mrs. Linton gave me a venomous glance, turned on her heel and strode into the kitchen.

Mrs. Jager sighed. "I believe I have lost my appetite too."

"Mrs. Jager, I'm sorry about this," I said. I felt like bursting into tears, yet I didn't wish to add to the unpleasantness. "I beg of you to believe me when I say I am innocent."

"If I didn't believe in your innocence," she replied, "you would not be in this house. May I also add that I do not believe you would be such a fool as to carry any effects of Vincent Seaton's around. The evidence would be too damning."

"I agree," I replied. "Yet such evidence has been found in my possession."

"I said before," Bruce broke in, "that it could have been placed there."

"By whom?" I asked in desperation.

"Yes, indeed," Mrs. Jager said, looking thoughtful. "By whom?"

"I don't know," Bruce said, making a disparaging gesture with his hands. "But I'm certain Melinda was unaware of the fact that Vincent Seaton's purse was in her possession."

"No matter," Mrs. Jager said, rising. "We'll go to the constable tomorrow and place the matter in his hands."

She left the room and there was no one left but Charity, Bruce and me. Charity placed a comforting arm around my shoulder, touched her cheek to mine and then arose.

"We all believe in your innocence except Fern," she said in that little-girl voice of hers. "And she won't ever because she says you killed Vincent."

My smile toward Charity was one of gratitude.

"I'm tired," she went on. "I'm going upstairs. You needn't come, Melinda. You've been through enough and you have to go to the village tomorrow."

"Thank you, Charity," I said gratefully. I too wished the privacy of my room, for I had much thinking to do. I had thought to escape the agony of what I'd been through by coming here, yet it seemed that I was living it all over again.

Charity left the room and Bruce walked around the table.

"I hope you won't let what happened to you tonight drive you out of here," he said. "I believe in you, as do both my aunts. As for Fern, I'd already prepared you for her before your arrival."

"You didn't tell me she'd been in love with Vincent," I replied quietly.

"She still is—with his memory. I remained silent about it because I felt you'd been through enough. I didn't dream she would tell you of the fact that he had tired of her."

"She didn't," I replied. "It was Charity who told me. She also tried to warn me to expect this from Fern. Will you excuse me, Bruce? I, too, am suddenly tired and I wish to go to my room."

"I understand," he replied kindly, and stepped aside so I might pass.

Alone in my suite, I wondered what I should do—indeed, what I could do. I knew, most of all, I wanted to find

55

out who had murdered Vincent Seaton. I could no longer stand the accusations. The inner pain I felt each time a finger was pointed at me had become so great, I could not further endure it.

Tears filmed my eyes and I blinked them away, feeling annoyed at such weakness. I had no time for tears. I must think of what to do. Then, slowly the answer came. Perhaps I could uncover a clue to the murderer of Vincent if I remained here.

To do so, I must retain the good graces of Mrs. Jager. She believed in my innocence and that was in my favor. As for Fern, her hatred of me was understandable. She had loved Vincent. Could she have killed him? Was I living in this mansion, close to the murderer of Vincent Seaton? Was it a coincidence that I had been hired as companion to Charity, or had it been done to insure my silence? And would I be done away with like Vincent?

I shuddered at the thought. Poor Vincent. A philanderer, but a charming one, who could sway the heart of any woman he chose. I had found him fascinating, been flattered by his attentions, believed myself in love with him.

I thought back to the times when he had told me he would stop by my house to take me for a ride or a stroll in the moonlight. I recalled that each time he didn't appear, the idea that he might be elsewhere with another woman had never occurred to me. Rather, I went to the Inn where he maintained a room, to inquire whether he might be ill. Instead, he was out and each time I returned to my little cottage, wondering as to his whereabouts. Then he told me the foolish tale of having been with a student who was lagging in his school grades. He was tutoring that student at the behest of his parents. I had believed him until the evening of his death, when I went to the schoolhouse to get some books. There, I overheard him quarreling with a woman. He had been cruel to her, taking no pains to conceal the fact that he had tired of her.

I'd left the schoolhouse quietly and started to return to my cottage. But I hadn't quite reached it when Vincent came, on foot, in pursuit. My exit hadn't been as silent as I'd thought. He'd pleaded with me to forget what I'd heard and when I told him there had been rumors of his seeing other young women, he denied it at first, then finally admitted it, swearing that, if I forgave him, he would see no other.

But I knew that even though he believed what he said at the moment, he was not the type of man who could be true to any woman. In my anger, I told him so, turned on my heel and sought the sanctuary of my cottage. I didn't know if my position at the school would now be forfeited, but if so, I would make the best of it. I would no longer be tricked by his blandishments. That was the last time I had seen him alive.

I heard him gallop past my house later that night and while I slept, he had met his death. How he managed to ride his horse with a bullet in him to my cottage, though bleeding to death, I will never know. Why he had come to me in his last moments, I didn't know either. Was it because he really loved me, or did he wish to tell me who had shot him? At any rate, the evidence showed that he'd fallen out of the saddle, crawled up onto my little porch and died, trying to awaken me.

I'd had some unpleasant hours in the custody of the constable who, fortunately, was trying to be fair and was bothered by too many holes in the theories that made me the killer. Then Bruce, as the village doctor, had taken a hand, and Lawyer Cecil Todd had come over to my side. However, a few hours after I was set free, the selectmen in the village voted that I no longer be employed as a teacher. I was forced to give up the little cottage that went with the position.

Finally, I went to bed. In the morning Delphine and I were going to the village, a journey I did not look forward to. I wanted to be rested for it, but I forced myself to read a short time before I blew out the lamp, to rid my mind of the unpleasantness of the dinner hour. Fortunately, I slept the night through and awoke early, refreshed and ready for the ordeal of facing the villagers.

When I reached the breakfast table, Bruce was there. He had finished his breakfast and after greeting me, continued to sip his coffee until I'd been served by one of the maids.

"I shall be in my village office from ten until two," he said. "If you need me, Melinda, please don't hesitate to come."

"Thank you, Bruce."

"I also want you to know that I don't for one moment believe you were aware that Vincent's purse was concealed in your baggage."

"Thank you, Bruce. I'm most eager to see the constable and relate everything to him, besides giving him Vincent's purse."

"I wonder if it's a wise thing, your going to the village," he mused.

"In heaven's name, why not?"

"I'm thinking of the villagers—of their antagonism toward you."

"I must risk that."

"In any case, Delphine would insist on going."

"I insist also, Bruce," I said, feeling a trace of irritation at his words. "In fact, it was I who suggested we do that very thing."

"I'm quite aware of it." .

"I dislike being made a spectacle of, as I was last night, and the quicker I get this over with, the more relieved I'll be."

Bruce set his cup down with such force, the liquid spilled over the side. "That was horrible and if I had my say, Tess would be asked to leave."

"I hope no such thing will happen." I smiled at his look of surprise. "I mean it, Bruce. I hope that as long as I am here, she will be. I'm rather suspicious of her. Can you blame me?"

"You don't think *she* killed Vincent," he exclaimed.

"Of course not. But she may know who did."

His eyes regarded me with amazement, but there was no further time for words, for just then Mrs. Jager swept into the room. She was already dressed and ready, but she had yet to breakfast, so I ate lightly, excused myself and returned upstairs to don my hat and gloves. I noted that Bruce remained behind, presumably to talk with his aunt, and I wondered if I would be the topic of discussion.

A sigh escaped me as I worked on one of my gloves. I was fond of Bruce—he'd been most kind to me—yet I was regarding him with suspicion. And how could I help it? In this very house, I'd as much as been accused of murder. Were they trying to make it seem I'd committed the wretched crime? I didn't know and I was determined to find out.

One of the gardeners drove us to the village in the carriage. He never uttered a word during the entire ride and though he bade Mrs. Jager a civil good morning when she approached the carriage, he turned his back on me. I was used to such treatment and pretended to take no notice. Instead, I sat back and feasted my eyes on the beauty of the countryside.

The journey to the village was uneventful and as we rode down the single street, I realized what a tawdry place it was. We were so isolated, and there were so few strangers about, that no one bothered to apply a paint brush or a repair-carpenter's hammer very often. The houses were, however, neat little places with fine lawns and many flower beds.

"Mrs. Jager," I said, "may I suggest that we first talk to Lawyer Todd? He warned me not to make any statements without his permission and I do believe that still applies."

"Cecil Todd is also my attorney," she said. "I'm very much in favor of his advice."

She called to the coachman and he turned off to stop the carriage directly in front of the two-story, wooden building on the second floor of which Lawyer Tood had his offices.

Cecil Todd was about fifty, I judged. A prematurely white-haired man, with a wide smile and a most pleasant manner. He was quite handsome and had a reputation as a fine attorney. I'd been most fortunate that he'd come to my side.

He shook hands with Mrs. Jager and provided the best chair in the office for her. Then he sat down and listened politely to my story.

"You have handled this exactly right." He addressed Mrs. Jager rather than me. "Melinda is still the prime suspect in this murder, though there isn't a shred of evidence to hold her on. But such things as the appearance of the purse in her room adds to the slim case the state now has."

"That purse was placed where my nosey housekeeper could find it," Delphine said. "Everyone knows that Tess never missed an opportunity to look over the baggage of any guest. I regard this only as an attempt to throw suspicion on Melinda and nothing else."

"Agreed," Mr. Todd nodded. "And a foolish one if you want my opinion, for now we can be even more certain that someone wishes Melinda to be blamed, and that means someone else must, therefore, be guilty. I think it best to give the purse to the constable with the entire story. If he makes too much trouble, send me word. He cannot hold Melinda on evidence as flimsy as has been developed so far, not even when it's backed up with the finding of this purse."

I left Mr. Todd, reassured and quite confident. We walked down the sidewalk toward the constable's home at the end of the street. On our way, we passed several ladies who bowed politely to Mrs. Jager, but deliberately ignored me. Delphine noticed it too and when Mrs. Larkin, who'd had two children in my class, continued on by us, Mrs. Jager took her by the arm and brought her to a halt.

"Mary Larkin, I'm surprised at your display of bad manners," Mrs. Jager said, her glance castigating the younger woman. "Or have you forgotten Miss Marston, who was a former teacher in our school, and a good one too?"

"I'm quite aware of Miss Marston's identity," Mrs. Larkin replied coldly. 'I only wish I were not. Good morning, Delphine."

"Well, of all the gall," Mrs. Jager exclaimed. "I am surprised at you, Mary."

But Mrs. Larkin had continued on her way.

Mrs. Jager shook her head in exasperation. "How cruel and unfair they are, to accuse you without proof."

"I'm used to it, Mrs. Jager. And I've decided that I cannot leave here until the murderer of Vincent Seaton is uncovered. I am sick at heart, having to live under this suspicion."

"Of course you are, my dear," she said consolingly. "But never fear, the person who committed the crime will one day be uncovered and when that day comes, I hope to walk along this street with you."

"Thank you, Mrs. Jager. You have no idea how grateful I am to have you for a friend. And how lucky I feel," I added with a smile.

"Just try not to worry too much," she said. "Bruce told me about the attack on you the first night you were here. I think we should mention it to the constable."

"Oh, please don't," I said impulsively. "We have enough to tell him now. I don't want to seem like a martyr."

"As you wish. Well, here we are, and if Theo Vendeveer, our worthy constable, makes any uncalled-for remarks, I shall give him a proper piece of my mind."

But Theo Vendeveer wasn't at home and wasn't expected until nightfall. There was a deputy in charge to whom we surrendered the purse and gave our story, which he painstakingly put down in a ledger. I had a feeling this whole journey was a wasted maneuver.

We walked back to where the carriage waited, this time without anyone snubbing me, and for a good reason. Everybody had deliberately gotten off the street so they wouldn't have to meet me and stand up to Mrs. Jager's wrath.

Neither of us spoke much until we were almost back to the Manor. Then Mrs. Jager explained to me the little scheme she had formulated as we rode, one I wished she had never thought of.

"I'm going to invite all the good ladies of the village to the Manor for tea. They won't dare refuse me because if they don't come, they'll never be invited again, and I may as well admit it, I'm society as far as the village is concerned. If I don't give parties now and then, no one does. I shall announce that the tea is in your honor."

"Oh, dear me, no," I exclaimed. "Please, Mrs. Jager. I couldn't stand it."

"You can and you will, my dear. I've seen what they've done to you in the village and it must stop. I'm the person who can put a halt to it. Besides, I'm fond of you and so, I might add, is Bruce. But then, I'm sure you're aware of that. He can scarcely turn his eyes from you to take his food from his plate."

I couldn't help giggling at her remark, so unexpected was it.

"There now," she said in satisfaction at my rise in spirits. "That's better. He told me this morning he asked you to sit for him."

"He did—yesterday. However, if you don't approve——"

"I do. I do most thoroughly. You're very beautiful. He's a fine artist and I know he will put his very heart in the painting. I have a feeling it will be his best work." She leaned over and patted my hands which rested in my lap. "Did you know he's had several villagers sit for him? He used to do some of his painting in his village office— or in a room just off it, I should say. He painted Alice Townsend and Emily Warner, Josh Anders and Sarah Miller——"

"I've seen some of his work," I said. "It's very good."

"Sometimes I think he likes painting more than the

61

practice of medicine, though he's an excellent doctor. Well, here we are, turning into the long drive. I always like this point on my return trip for I have my best look at the Manor. Some think it an ugly monstrosity of a place, but I think it's one of the most perfect places I have ever seen. To me, it's absolutely beautiful."

I didn't reply and she looked at me in a slightly annoyed fashion, but I was hardly aware of it for my mind was on something else—something just a bit too horrible to give voice to.

Bruce had painted several villagers, as his aunt had just pointed out, and among them the four she'd named. All four had been young, attractive people—and all were now dead. All had died violently, one way or another. Alice Townsend had been found drowned in a rather shallow pond just outside of town. Emily Warner had been discovered dead by the side of the road, apparently the victim of a runaway horse and carriage, though none was ever reported. Josh Anders had set out poison to thin out woodchucks on the farm his father ran and somehow Josh had swallowed some of the poison. Sarah Miller had been found hanging in Sycamore Grove, a picnic grounds used by the village. It was obviously a suicide, but no motive for it had ever been discovered.

They'd all died shortly after having posed for Bruce. It could be coincidental, and likely was, but it did seem that sitting for a portrait by artist Bruce Erskine was, to say the least, dangerous.

FIVE

After lunch, I attempted to interest Charity in a game of croquet, but she refused to play and expressed a desire only to lie down and have a nap. I accompanied her to the door of her room and continued on to my own, for I still had many invitations to write and they occupied me until I noticed the clock on the mantel over the fireplace. It was a quarter of three. I dried my pen with a wiper, set the desk in order and retired to the bathroom to wash the ink off my fingers.

I decided to wear the dress I'd donned for dinner last night. It was my most becoming and my newest. My hair was still in order, for I wore it with the bun coiled low on my neck and, on impulse, I placed a silk flower in it. The effect was rather daring for me and, I thought, quite gay, but it seemed to lift my spirits and I was sure Bruce would not object.

Yet, as I left my room for his studio, I couldn't help thinking of those four young people whose portraits he'd painted and all of whom were now dead. If they had died a natural death, I would not have dwelt on it, but of the four, three deaths had been accidental and one a suicide. It seemed strange and, I had to admit, rather frightening. Yet my hand didn't falter as it raised to knock lightly on his open door, for I was most eager to be in this gentleman's company. I supposed it was because he'd shown me both kindness and sympathy from the moment he first spoke to me, the night Vincent's body was found on my porch.

I was being unfair when I allowed myself to think about what had happened to those four unfortunate subjects who had sat for him. The fate they subsequently suffered could be nothing but pure coincidence.

Bruce came to meet me, one hand extended to clasp mine. A warm glow of gratitude flowed through me at his touch.

"I thought you might not come," he said quietly, his eyes studying me.

"Such a thought never occurred to me," I replied in surprise.

"I didn't know whether the ordeal of this morning was too much for you."

"It was no ordeal, except for the snub I received from one of the villagers. However, it was hardly unexpected."

"Mrs. Larkin," Bruce said, nodding. "My aunt told me about the unpleasantness. She was quite irate about the incident."

"Did she also tell you she is giving a tea, inviting the women of the village, to force them to accept me?"

"Yes." He'd led me over to the high-backed chair which was now on a platform and he assisted me onto it. "She could speak of nothing else."

"Do you think it wise," I asked him bluntly, "in view of what happened?"

He thought a moment. "I believe her intentions are of the best, but I think it would have been wiser to wait until more time passed."

"Wiser still to wait until Vincent's murderer was discovered."

"Yes," he agreed. "But my aunt is a very headstrong woman. She was angered by the treatment you received this morning. She is also a very powerful woman in the village and she believes that since she has accepted you, the villagers must also."

I sat down and he tilted my head at the proper angle as he spoke. The high-backed chair was arranged so the afternoon sunlight would cut through the room, directly behind me. His canvas was set up nearby; a palette was ready as well as his several brushes.

"Is that position uncomfortable?" he asked.

"Not in the least." Then, going back to the subject under discussion, I said, "I fear, in this case, your aunt is going to be sadly mistaken and I am going to be in for a very hard time."

"My dear," his hands cupped my face, "you have a tremendous amount of courage. You displayed it during the investigation. I'm sure you will weather the afternoon. Remember, you're not alone. I'm proud to be your friend. At least, I hope you consider me as such."

"Oh, I do, I do," I exclaimed. "If it hadn't been for you, I doubt I'd have been able to endure such an ordeal."

A smile touched his lips. "Thank you, Melinda. I'fear though, I haven't been completely honest with you."

My eyes widened in puzzlement. "What do you mean?"

"I don't just like you. I don't just think of you as a friend. I'm very fond of you. It goes even deeper than that, but I don't wish to frighten you so that you'll jump out of this chair, run from the studio and leave this house."

It was my turn to smile. "I shan't. Your words please me, though they come as a surprise."

"I wasn't aware I was so good at keeping a secret. You see, I love you, my dear. I've loved you for a long time. Oh, I saw you with Vincent and I knew him for the roué he was and it made my blood boil to know he was deceiving you. Strange that it was his untimely death which brought us together. Of course," he added, "I don't know in what regard you hold me."

"Oh, Bruce," I said and I wondered if he could feel the pulse throbbing in my temples, for his hands still enclosed my face, "you are a very dear man. And while I have so far refused to admit it, even to myself, I am very fond of you. But it can go no further. Not while I'm suspected of Vincent Seaton's murder."

His eyes disputed my words as his head lowered and I know he was about to kiss me. Whether I would have allowed him to, I don't know, but possibly, to discourage such an act, my eyes flicked from his face to glance over his shoulder. They widened in sudden horror as the face of Alice Townsend, a sad-eyed girl with delicate features and blond hair, stared at me from the canvas.

Bruce sensed the magic of the moment was gone and his hands dropped from my face as he noted the direction of my gaze. "That girl's life was very tragic. She's dead, you know."

"I know," I replied, unable to take my eyes from the portrait. "She was much too young and beautiful to die."

"Yes—not only Alice, but the others. Four subjects who sat for me died violent deaths—or did you know?"

"I . . . heard about it."

"If the people in the village wish to suspect someone, they ought to look to me. I had four models die violently. All within a few months. I was so depressed by it, I—gave up painting portraits after Sarah Miller's death. I didn't want to paint anyone else. But no, that isn't exactly true. I wanted to paint you even before the others sat for me, but the opportunity never presented itself. What I mean is, I didn't want to do any more portrait work until the day I brought you here and suddenly the urge to paint overwhelmed me once again. But if the thought of my having painted those unfortunate people worries you, causes you to be fearful, perhaps we shouldn't begin, Melinda."

"No—I don't believe your painting them had anything to do with their deaths. It was unfortunate coincidence. I'll be honored to have you paint my portrait."

"There is yet another reason why you may not wish to sit for me," he said and he was looking straight at me and, once again, warmth crept into his eyes and I knew what he was going to say. "We'll be together often and for rather extended periods of time—do you know what I'm about to say?"

"I'd rather not guess," I replied, and though my voice was calm, my heart was pounding madly.

"Then I shall tell you. I've been in love with you since the first time I saw you. I will be frank to admit I was jealous of Vincent Seaton, though I was appalled at his violent death. Regardless of what he was, he didn't deserve that."

"Apparently, someone thought otherwise," I observed.

"In any case, now you know my feelings. I shan't press you at this time, but I hope with all my being that, one day soon, your eyes will tell me that my love for you is not in vain."

My heart was urging me to cry out, to tell this man how I felt about him. It wasn't just gratitude. I knew it the moment his hands enclosed my face. It went far deeper than that. It was love. Such love as I had never known and had no right to express at this time. He stood, looking down at me, waiting for me to speak and I knew that after revealing his love for me, he was deserving of an answer.

"Bruce," I said, "it would be very easy to love you. You've been kind, helpful——"

"I don't want your gratitude," he said and there was an urgency to his words as he added, "Could you love me?"

"Yes," I replied with a frankness that amazed me. "But I will not let myself think of you in that regard so long as I am held suspect by all, for miles around."

He smiled. "Just so I can hope. I'll endeavor to be patient, but remember, I am a man and I have waited a long time to tell you that I love you."

only been here six months," I reminded him, and my smile chided him. "Hadn't you better start to paint before the day is too far gone?"

He chuckled. "How like a woman. Always so practical. Very well. You've lost the pose so I must once again place your head in the proper position."

I feared Bruce's touch—what it might do to me. But he was now the artist and his eyes regarded me objectively as his hands gently turned my head in the position he wanted. He stepped back, studied my profile, came toward me and raised my chin slightly.

"This is going to be a portrait of your head only. A semi-profile to capture the lines of your face. I hope to do several of you, Melinda, if I may."

"I'm flattered at your interest," I replied.

Again he lifted up my chin slightly, then moved over to the canvas and began to sketch rapidly with charcoal. He worked swiftly, but before long I could feel my neck muscles begin to protest, for they were unused to this somewhat awkward position. I finally had to beg a recess. Bruce laid down his charcoal and filled one of the several pipes on the table. He lit it and the aromatic tobacco was pleasant to smell. He sat down, draping himself comfortably in one of the short, round-backed chairs he likely used to pose some of his subjects.

"Just what happened in the village today?" he asked. "My aunt spoke only of the incident with Mrs. Larkin."

"Your aunt and I talked to Cecil Todd and he thought the idea of turning the purse over to the constable a good one. But the constable wasn't at home so we gave it to one of his deputies with a full statement. I do hope it will help him."

"I hope so. He's a fair-minded man."

"Bruce," I asked, frowning at the thought I was about to express, "do you think Mrs. Linton lied when she said the wallet fell out of one of my bags?"

"I wish I could say I did, but I've never known of her to tell an untruth. To snoop—yes, but not lie. You forget last night I said it could have been placed in your bag."

"But by whom? Someone in this house? Do you believe the murderer is here?"

"Good God, no!" Bruce exclaimed. He set down his pipe, arose and started to pace back and forth. "There's only Fern and I'd stake my life on the fact that she

67

wouldn't kill anybody. She's selfish, has a vitriolic ⌐
but a murderess—no!"

"Someone put it there.

"Little question about that. Shall we go back to work?"

He moved to his canvas, picked up his palette and I resumed the pose. I spent another hour in that uncomfortable position until I thought I'd not be able to move my neck again.

Finally, Bruce set down his palette. "That's it for today."

I relaxed, moving my neck and shoulders to ease the tired muscles. Bruce remained behind to clean his brushes, but he took care to cover the portrait so I could not see what he'd accomplished.

I went directly to my room to spend the time until dinner writing more invitations. I hoped to complete them by tonight before I retired for I wanted them to be posted tomorrow. However, I would have to enlist Charity's cooperation in signing them.

With an eye on the clock, I wrote steadily until there was just enough time for Charity to sign several of the invitations. I gathered them up, brought them to her room and knocked on the door. I had to knock repeatedly and when she finally answered, her eyes were still befogged with sleep.

"Good gracious, Charity, I'd hoped you'd be dressed for dinner." I held up the invitations. "You still have many of these to sign."

"You do it for me, Melinda," she replied, moving lazily toward the bedroom. "My hand is tired already from signing so many."

Mine was tired from writing, but I felt that to be unimportant. I had to help her dress and do up her hair. We were barely downstairs and in our chairs before Delphine strode into the room, to be seated by Bruce, and, as if on signal, dinner began with the appearance of Mrs. Linton, followed by two waitresses carrying heavily-laden trays.

It was an unusually lively dinner, with the conversation around the subject of impressing the village women at the tea which would be held the day after tomorrow. Delphine had already sent two of the gardeners into the village to deliver the invitations.

"I want this to be quite a grand thing," Delphine said. "In its way, as grand as the dinner-ball next week. Melinda, you have a tea dress? Something quite elaborate, to impress these simple women."

My smile was embarrassed. "I fear the dress I am wearing is my best."

"Fern, you have many afternoon dresses. You are Melinda's size. You must loan her your choicest tea gown. Do you heed me now, Fern? Your very best, and I know which it is, so don't bring her one of your older ones."

"Yes, Auntie," Fern said obediently, but the antagonism in her eyes as they met mine was evidence of how much she resented that order. I wished Delphine had never given it.

"Tess," Delphine called the housekeeper to her side. "You will outdo yourself in seeing that cook prepares unusual salads and sandwiches. None of those dainty things like cucumber or watercress sandwiches. These village women work hard and like substantial food. There should be mountains of dessert, the richer the better, and strong coffee. Everything is to be served on the gold service. It is certain to impress them. Charity, I'll expect you to look your best and so must you, Fern. I also expect you to make a display of cordiality toward Melinda."

"Delphine," Charity said shyly, "I love Melinda. She's my friend. The only one I've got. I couldn't do without her now."

The smile Charity bestowed on me left no doubt as to the warmth of regard in which she held me. I returned the smile, but it left my face quickly as I looked across the table at Fern, for her glance, directed at me, was venomous.

I said, "I'd rather not borrow a dress from Fern. I'd prefer to wear what I have, even though it is quite a simple frock."

"Nonsense, my dear, I'll hear of no change in my plans," Mrs. Jager stated firmly. "Fern will bring you her best tea gown and you will wear it. It should fit perfectly, as you are identical in size."

"But there the identity ceases," Bruce broke in. "It's about time my sister grew up. I'm quite tired of her nastiness and I think it would be a good idea if she went on vacation somewhere."

"I intend to," Fern replied tartly, "but not while Miss Marston is an occupant in this house." She directed her words to me. "I will obey my aunt and I will be courteous to you—my manner even friendly—but remember, I am doing so only because I've been ordered."

"I shall remember," I said quietly, meeting her gaze. "I would also like to state that I feel that though Mrs. Jager's intentions are of the highest in having this tea, she is making a sad mistake, for I knew I will not be accepted by the villagers."

"You must face up to them, my dear," Mrs. Jager said. "Never admit defeat. I never have and because I haven't, I am always the victor. Life is a challenge which we must all meet. If we run from it, we shall end up as miserable cowards. You, Melinda, are not a coward. You proved that in the village. Here, you are among friends and, believe me, we will lend you moral support."

"You see, Melinda," Bruce said, smiling encouragement, "Aunt Delphine is going to do her best to break down the prejudice that exists against you in the village."

"Not only in the village," I replied. "I fear that, for miles around, I am the only suspect."

"People forget," Mrs. Jager assured me.

"Not where a murder is concerned," I replied.

"My dear," Mrs. Jager leaned forward as if to impress me with what she was about to say, "let us have no further talk of murder. It serves only to depress you. Do your best to drive the tragedy from your mind. After all, it isn't as if you loved the man at the time of his death—or did you?"

"I—thought I did," I said quietly. "But now I realize I mistook gratitude for love."

"An easy matter to do in one so young," she said. "And one thing more. I don't wish that rounder's name to be mentioned at the tea. I'm certain if we do our part, we will remove all prejudice from Melinda by the time those ladies depart the Manor."

I wished I were as sure. I sat back and listened quietly as Delphine spoke of the tea and of what she intended to do, to insure its success. Through it all, Bruce's eyes never left my face. I was heartened by the warmth and tenderness in them and, somehow, I felt strengthened by it. Charity broke in now and then with suggestions which Mrs. Jager listened to politely, but due to their impracticability, I doubted she would adopt them. One idea was to have Japanese lanterns—which would be lit—in the formal gardens in the afternoon.

Fern sniffed, but sat silent and stony-faced. I got the

idea that she knew better than to defy her aunt by scoffing at or belittling Charity in any way.

It was late when dinner was over and just as we were about to leave, a messenger arrived from the village. It was an emergency call for Bruce. Mrs. Jager frowned slightly at the intrusion, then asked him if he had his key and matches with him for use on his return. When he replied he had, she turned to me, explaining she was against having any lamps burning after everyone had retired because of the fear of fire. She smiled tolerantly at her nephew as she added that when he went out on a night call, it might be daylight before he returned.

I prepared for bed and finished my book, but I was not yet tired enough for sleep. I'd noticed that new issues of *Woman's Home Companion* and *Godey's Book* had arrived in the mail and were on the table in the family drawing room. While I had no great desire to be abroad alone in this huge old house, I was curious to view those magazines, so I found my slippers, my wrapper and lit a candle.

I left my rooms and moved quietly along the hall so as not to disturb anyone. I started down the steps but I paused as I reached the mid-section where the two branches joined into the wide and outstandingly beautiful staircase to the entrance hall.

I should have used a lamp, for the house was closed for the night and there were no lights downstairs. A candle was feeble illumination in this big house. But I knew where the magazines were so I gathered up my courage and kept going.

I had entered the drawing room and was passing the windows when I heard the sharp crack of dry branches just outside. I quickly shaded the candle from the window and moved toward it. This was an extremely dark night and I could see nothing. But I had heard someone moving out there. It could have been an animal, but I thought from the way the branch cracked, it was caused by the sudden weight of a human being.

I was growing more and more apprehensive as I stood peering out, for I became aware of the creaks and groans all old houses develop, though the Manor seemed to have more than an ordinary share. A more active imagination than mine could have conjured up goblins and specters all through the darkness of the first floor.

I moved away from the window, found the magazines,

seized them and, by serious effort, kept myself from running back upstairs. I suddenly hated this house. Lavish though it was, it frightened me. I took measured steps instead and it wasn't until I reached the entrance hall that once again I heard the cracking of branches, this time close to the front entrance.

I moved up to the door immediately. It was flanked by two long, narrow windows, which were curtained, but I moved the curtain of one aside and peered out in time to see a dark, unidentifiable form slip past the porch and head for the north side of the house where he was swallowed up by darkness and shrubbery. So I hadn't been mistaken. Someone was prowling about. For a moment I was tempted to open the door to see if I could catch a further glimpse of whoever it was, but I thought better of it. I certainly did not want a repetition of last night's adventure. I thought of summoning Bruce, then recalled he was not in the house, but out on an emergency call. The thought of his absence appalled me.

The idea of going to Mrs. Jager occurred to me, but by the time I got there, the prowler could have disappeared and I would seem a fool. Besides, even if he were still on the premises, what could she, a woman in her fifties, do?

As for Charity, telling her about someone skulking around the estate would only make her whimper and draw her head further beneath the covers. She'd be fearful the entire night, wouldn't sleep, and would probably spend the following day in bed instead of just the afternoon. It would be much kinder not to worry her.

I knew Fern would have the courage to search the grounds with me, but I doubted she would give me the satisfaction of doing so. Her attitude would be one of condescending contempt. As for her staunch ally, Mrs. Linton, I'd not go near her. She'd accuse me of trying to throw suspicion away from myself, by frightening everyone.

In the sanctuary of my room once again, I lit lamps and, setting down the magazines, I returned to the invitations, hoping work would quiet my nerves and it did serve to take my mind off my loneliness and fears.

It was almost two hours before I'd finished, but at last the final address was placed on the envelope, and it was sealed and stamped. Instead of feeling relieved the chore was ended, I shuddered at the thought of the affair, for I knew I would be forced to undergo the humiliation that was bound to occur at the tea. Despite Mrs. Jager's beliefs, I knew I was in as deep disgrace as if I were a scarlet woman.

I sat back, wearily rubbed my eyes and stretched my arms over my head in an effort to relax, but to no effect. I was still frightened over having seen the figure on the grounds, wondering what it might portend. I was aware of the quickened beat of my heart and the slightest creaking of the house made me jump. The terror which I felt was one which had seemed to build up from deep within me, try as I might, I could not shake it off.

I forced myself to go into the darkened bedroom and look out the windows. I could not be seen and my eyes could slowly traverse the extensive grounds. Nothing human seemed to move and I told myself my fears were silly. Two tables flanked my bed and I placed a lamp on each one.

There were still two lamps burning in the sitting room, but I decided to leave them lit until I was ready for sleep. I wondered if it would come this night. I picked up one of the magazines and, propping myself up on my pillows, I started to read, trying to free my mind of all the dire thoughts and emotions which had taken possession of me.

I read for well over an hour and still didn't feel sleepy. I'd left my watch on the bureau so I slipped out of bed to get it. I was quite amazed to learn it was after one. No wonder the household was shrouded in such deep silence. Everyone must have been asleep for hours.

I started another story, but I couldn't get interested in it. I knew I had to get out of bed once more and blow out the lamps in the sitting room. Their supply of oil was low and they'd hardly burn until morning. I surely didn't want the task of cleaning lamp chimneys, because they had blackened, but I would have, rather than admit I'd been afraid to sleep in the dark. Also, I was aware of Mrs. Jager's rule of no lamps burning when all occupants of the house had retired. She was, obviously, afraid of fire and I could understand her apprehension.

Shrugging off my fear of the dark, I resolutely threw aside the covers and made my way to the sitting room. There I blew out the lamps and returned to the bedroom, taking each step with deliberate slowness. Now I had but the two bedside lamps burning. I settled down to finish the magazine, even reading the pages on baby care, while my ears were attuned for the first sounds of Bruce returning from his case. It was strange how I knew I'd feel much better, once he was in the house.

If I didn't sleep, this was going to be a very long night and I dreaded the thoughts of it. Finally, telling myself I was an idiot, I blew out both lamps and lay down, attempting to free my mind of all unpleasantness.

Perhaps, in the next few moments, I would have been successful in drifting off, for an exhausting weakness had set in as a result of my mental turmoil, but just then a sound occurred which made every nerve in my body tighten.

It was a light rattling noise, as if some object had struck one of my bedroom windows. Immediately, I thought of Bruce and a flood of relief swept through me. Without thinking of any danger to myself, I threw off the covers and hurried to one of the windows which looked out onto the front of the estate.

My spirits lifted as I saw a man about twenty yards from the front of the house. He had an arm raised and, with long sweeping motions, was beckoning for me to come to him. But then I realized it wasn't Bruce.

Sudden curiosity overcame my fear and as my eyes focused on the figure in the darkness, I recognized this person and I covered my mouth with my hand to hold back the cry which almost escaped me.

There could be no mistaking the thin, gaunt figure of Billy Cornell. The black stocking cap covered his head. Simple Billy, some of the villagers had called him. I wondered just how simple he was—and just how harmless, for I suspected he might be the man who had tried to strangle me.

Yet he was urging me to come out. I felt a sudden surge of anger toward this young man which superseded my fear. I wished to see his face. I wanted to ask him some questions. But to do so, I must go downstairs, leave the safety of the house and, perhaps, risk my life. Yet suddenly, it became of the utmost importance for me to do so.

I donned my wrapper, got into my slippers and lit a lamp. I raised it at the window as a signal that I was on my way and, as if he understood, he stopped beckoning to me. I left my rooms and moved quietly along the corridor and down the stairway.

It wasn't until I reached the front door that I hesitated,

for I realized then that it was quite possible I was placing myself in considerable peril. Billy could be luring me out of doors to kill me. But this time I would be prepared. I had strong lungs and I would scream mightily should he attempt to lay a hand on me. My mind made up, I placed the lamp on the table, turned the knob, made certain the door was unlocked and stepped outside.

I moved to the edge of the porch, looked around, but there wasn't a sign of Billy. Then I went down the steps. Not even a night sound disturbed the terrifying quiet and there was no evidence that another human being was even near me.

"Billy," I called softly. "Billy—I'm here. What do you want?"

Nothing answered me but the stillness of the night. I moved about, refusing to panic, hoping the young man would come forward. I was careful to remain in the center of the path so that he could not surprise me by suddenly appearing from behind a bush. I would not be taken unawares this time.

A soft sigh of despair escaped me and I turned to retrace my steps to the house when I heard a sound—not terrifying or ear-shattering, yet it set my nerves on edge. I could not believe my ears, yet I knew it wasn't the rustle of leaves, for no breeze stirred. What I heard was the notes of an organ being played very, very softly.

My hand clutched my wrapper at the region of my heart, as if by doing so I could still its wild beating. I wanted to seek the sanctuary of the house, for the sound was eerie in this midnight stillness, yet almost without my being aware of it, I began to move in the direction of the chapel. And as I did so, the music became clearer, yet it was still barely discernible—as if whoever played didn't wish to disturb those sleeping in the house.

I wondered if I was losing my mind. I wondered if the music I heard was real. Before, when I'd mentioned it, no one at the house had believed me, including Bruce. Now I would see for myself. I had to know. *I had to know.*

SIX

I felt that I must go to the chapel. If I could see someone playing that organ, if I could identify that person, then perhaps I'd be taken more seriously.

Also, there was the matter of Billy Cornell. He'd wanted me for some reason, but by the time I came out to meet him, he'd vanished. Then the organ began playing. Was that why he'd urged me to come out? Was it he who played the organ? I doubted that Billy had the mental ability to play anything, even a tissue on a comb, but the music was so soft that I couldn't tell if it was really music or just someone toying with the keys. Billy could do that easily enough.

Curiosity overcame my fear as the music continued, and I walked faster. I knew if I really saw someone at that organ, I'd feel far easier in mind.

Actually, I told myself, there was little to be afraid of. Just someone who wanted to play an organ and chose to do so in the middle of the night. It might even be Fern.

I had entered the extremely dark portions of the path and some of my assurance left me, for it was near there that I'd been attacked. Perhaps all of this, Billy awakening me, beckoning to me, the playing of the organ, was only meant to lure me into position for another assault. I came to an abrupt stop to listen, but except for the low drone of the organ I could hear nothing. In a few seconds I'd see the chapel and, for some strange reason, the thought repelled me. I wanted to turn and run away.

The path curved, straightened and there it was. The chapel! But not as I'd expected it, not closed up with only faint light through one or two of the front stained-glass windows.

The double doors were wide open. Light streamed out and it seemed that every candle in the chapel had been lit. The windows gleamed in their myriad colors. The organ music was still soft, but plainer now that I was this close. There was substance to it, a melody which I instantly recognized as Mendelssohn's Wedding March!

My steps slowed to a crawl. Between me and that chapel

was a thick curtain of fear which I doubted I could penetrate. There was something in that chaped meant for me to see, but I didn't wish to see it. Instinct warned me to turn and run for my very life.

Perhaps that's what I would have done, but at that moment Billy appeared fifty feet ahead of me. The light was full on him as he stepped into the path from the brush so there was no doubting his identity this time.

He hadn't seen me and he walked slowly toward the open chapel doors as if he too were irresistibly drawn there. It occurred to me then that Billy wasn't guilty of the organ playing at least. Someone else was in there.

"Billy!" I said sharply.

He whirled about. He wasn't close enough for me to detect the marks of any scratches on his face and there'd have been precious little opportunity to do so anyway, for he leaped off the path into the brush.

To me, it seemed more important to find him than to investigate the chapel. I had a conviction that Billy could supply all the answers I required and he'd be a witness to my story. So I went after him.

The area was well lighted by the chapel windows. Billy bobbed up once, but well to my left and even further ahead of me. I didn't call to him again but rushed after him. He was near the rear of the chapel now and I had a perfectly good look at him for an instant. Then he just seemed to be swallowed up by the earth.

When I reached the spot, there wasn't the slightest sign of him, and yet if he'd gone plunging through the very thick brush at this point, I should have heard him. I searched for a few minutes and then gave up. At least I still had the occupant of the chapel, for the organ hadn't stopped playing.

I felt that there really wasn't much to fear. Certainly Billy had been more of a potential danger than someone who was so devoted to organ music that he played in the middle of the night on an organ which he had no business using.

As I neared the front of the chapel, the music stopped very abruptly. It had been repeating the Wedding March, but it was cut off in the middle of it. Now an intense silence settled upon the night. Nothing stirred, I couldn't even hear the breeze. The chapel stood there, fully illuminated, asking me to enter, but my feeling toward the chapel had changed. It was now one of fear.

There was something inside meant for me to see, but why at this unseemly hour of the night under such terrifying conditions? I continued on, just as I knew I'd be compelled to do. I mounted the few steps to the doors and there I stopped.

The chapel was quite well filled. The forward pews contained about a score of people and there was an assembly of persons before the altar. It was a bright and cheerful scene on the surface, but there was something wrong. The awful stillness! With all these people present, someone should have coughed, or whispered, or shifted about. The people before the altar seemed to be frozen in place, yet all wore their finest and the women's gowns were of cheerful colors and rich materials.

I took a few tentative steps down the center aisle. The silence was the worst I had to endure. I reached a point away from the low ceiling of the organ loft and now the stained glass lent even more color to the scene. I turned and looked up at the loft. Two tall candles were placed on either side of the organ. They burned quietly. There was no one at the organ.

I moved on until I came to the first members of the congregation. I could see now that this was a wedding. Three bridesmaids stood waiting, dressed in identical pale blue gowns.

I looked closely at the man seated at the end of the pew. Now it was possible to see that it wasn't a man, but a wax image of one. The face was lifelike enough to fool anyone from a dozen feet away. The body of the effigy was well and carefully dressed. The woman beside him was likewise only a dummy, as were all the rest of this weird congregation.

The uncanny stillness, the silent inanimate congregation, all brought upon me a terror such as I had never before known. I made myself continue on to the scene before the altar. The groom was there and so was the best man, but no bride. The faces of these principal figures were turned toward the altar and, therefore, away from me. I was urged on by the compelling necessity to see who they were. I walked between them, much as the bride would have, had she appeared. I looked at the lovely faces of the bridesmaids and I knew each one. I'd seen them, spoken to them, liked them. These were the likenesses of Alice Townsend, Emily Warner and Sarah Miller. I'd been to their funerals. They'd all been painted by Bruce and they had all died by violence.

Stunned, I forced myself to look at the best man, though I knew very well he would be Josh Anders, also a subject of Bruce's brush and also dead violently.

There was yet the groom. I looked into the exact, terrifyingly real looking face of a man I once thought I'd loved and for whose murder I was still under suspicion.

The sight of Vincent Seaton's image broke whatever reserve of courage I still possessed. He had that same half-smile on his face. Handsome, debonair, devil-may-care Vincent who now lay cold and dead in his grave; yet seemed alive and still eager for life, so perfect was the image.

I covered my mouth with my hands to still the cry of terror which seemed to well from deep within me and I stood, motionless, on the altar, facing the assembly of silent, lifeless effigies. I felt as cold as winter and yet I could feel beads of perspiration forming on my forehead and beginning to flow down my face. My throat was dry, my mouth agape, my lips trembling. A convulsive shiver ran through my whole body.

I was the only living being here! I was the victim of some macabre travesty on life and death. Was this done to frighten me? If so, the perpetrator of this deed had succeeded. I had to get out of here before I became bereft of my senses. But to leave, I had to walk down that aisle between those ghostly replicas of humans—the ghostly guests of this ghostly wedding. I had the feeling that they were all looking at me, waiting to see what I'd do, laughing at me and daring me to pass them.

Then suddenly, I remembered the scene wasn't complete. There was no bride! Was I the intended? But I was alive! These dummies were of dead people—all painted by Bruce! Bruce—who was now painting my portrait. Was I scheduled for a violent death? Had I been tricked out of the house to view this lurid scene so that I would know what was in store for me? What further misery awaited me?

I took a deep breath and started to move from the altar. It took all my courage and my legs trembled so that my steps wavered. I was terrified of those dummies. It was as if I feared they would come to life, tear me limb from limb, and thus defile this holy chapel. Yet nothing moved. The only sound was the slithering of my slippers against the wooden floor. I stepped down from the altar, passed the bridesmaids, moved along the aisle between the congregation. I think the silence was the worst. I finally reached a point halfway to the still wide-open double doors. I thought that if they swung shut, trapping me in here with this weird assembly, I would surely lose my mind in a moment's time. The very thought spurred my nerves into action, my muscles into movement. My reason returned and with it, a desire to escape this eerie scene. I began to run.

I ran out of that chapel and into the night without once looking back—I dared not. I had escaped. From what horror I wasn't sure, but I was free.

I kept running along the path. I started to scream. Screams that taxed my lungs to their capacity, and I kept on running until I was at the door, which I had left unlocked.

I ran into the house and reeled over to the staircase, leaning against it, using it as a support to hold me up, no longer screaming, but sobbing hysterically. Yet it was with an inner sense of relief that I glimpsed someone moving swiftly down the stairs, holding a candelabrum.

And then, though I felt a momentary relief, it swiftly fled as I beheld Fern, setting down the candle and coming toward me. She was wearing only her nightdress, her feet were bare and her lovely hair hung almost to her waist.

"What is it, Melinda?" she exclaimed, and her voice was filled with concern.

"Get away from me!" I screamed. "Get away from me! How could you do such a thing to me? How could you? How horrible you are, Fern! I know you hate me, but I never believed you would be so cruel!" My throat was tightened from the shock of what I'd been through and it made my voice high and distorted.

"What are you talking about?" she asked. Even in my anguish I thought, *what a consummate actress you are— thinking up a scheme to frighten me to death, then pretending concern.*

"Get away from me!" I shrieked again. "Get away from me! I don't want you near me!"

"What is it, my dear?" It was Mrs. Jager who stood at

my side. She was carrying a lamp and genuine shock was on her features.

I suppose I did frighten her, but I couldn't stop babbling, the words spilling from me, shrill, loud and distorted. Finally, she raised a hand and slapped me resoundingly across the face. The force of it threw my head to one side, but the pain of the blow brought me out of that terrible hysteria which gripped me.

"The chapel," I said. "Full of—of dummies. Of dead people—dummies of dead people. . . . It's lit up. . . . Fern—played the—wedding march. . . . It was Fern—trying to frighten me."

Mrs. Jager turned to Fern, who had backed away from me. "What is she talking about?" she asked her niece.

"I don't know, Aunt," Fern exclaimed. "Truly, I don't know."

"Were you in the chapel?" Mrs. Jager asked sternly.

"I was not," Fern replied. "I was sound asleep and was awakened by Melinda's horrible screaming."

"I think the girl's daft," Mrs. Linton said. Her short hair was braided so tightly that the braids stuck out on the sides of her head and quivered with her every word. "She's lost her wits, that's what happened."

Charity moved over to me and she seemed on the verge of tears. "What happened, Melinda? What did Fern do to you?"

"I did nothing," Fern stated. But strangely, there was no anger in her voice, rather a plea to be believed. However, I refused to glance at her.

Mrs. Jager set down the lamp, came over to me and placed an arm around my shoulder. "Try to tell us what happened. Or what you believe happened.'

"I saw Billy Cornell on the estate. He threw a stone at my window to attract my attention and beckoned for me to come out. I did and, in trying to find him, I heard organ music. I lost Billy, but on my way to the chapel, which I saw was lit, I saw him again and chased him, but he eluded me. Then I went into the chapel—" I paused and as my mind recalled what I'd seen, I covered my face with my hands.

"Go on, my dear," Mrs. Jager said softly.

"Vincent Seaton was there and Alice Townsend, and Emily Warner, Josh Anders, Sarah Miller. Dead—all dead. But they were there. Wax images of them were there and

Vincent was dressed as the bridegroom. The bride wasn't present. Josh was best man—all of them dead. And there was a congregation—many people. All figures seated there as if alive."

"Tess," Delphine said, "prepare a glass of warm milk and add a dollop of brandy to it. Right away!"

Tess nodded and scampered off. Charity backed away from me, obviously frightened by the look on my face or possibly my disheveled appearance. Fern remained as calm as Mrs. Jager. Perhaps even calmer.

"Melinda, are you certain of what you're saying?" Mrs. Jager asked.

"I know—I know. . . . All of this I saw. Moments ago. It's the truth. You can see for yourself. They're all there. I don't understand it, but that's what happened."

Charity suddenly cried out. "Someone's coming—Delphine, don't let anybody in. Don't let anyone in the house. We'll be murdered!"

Mrs. Jager went to one of the windows beside the door. "Thank heavens," she said, "it's Bruce." She opened the door. Bruce, leading his horse, was going to the stables with the animal, but when Mrs. Jager summoned him, he quickly tied the horse and hurried inside.

He needed but a look at me to know something was very wrong. He came over to me, placed an arm around me and gently led me to a chair. I sat down gratefully and he turned to the others.

"What is going on?" he demanded.

Fern said, "We don't really know, Bruce. I heard Melinda scream and I came downstairs to find her beside herself with terror. Mrs. Linton joined me and so did Aunt Delphine and Charity. When Melinda was able to make herself understood, she told us someone was in the chapel. The organ was playing and—and—the people in there were wax figures. . . . She blames me, but I don't know what she's talking about."

Bruce looked down at me and in a gesture of encouragement he took one of my hands in his. "Melinda, please tell me what happened to you. Everything!"

Now that he was close by, I felt my courage return and I started to talk, telling in detail all that had happened since the moment I heard the stone—thrown by Bill Cornell—against my bedroom window. I described the wax figures in the chapel, told of the organ music and was pleased to see Bruce's glance shift accusingly to Fern. She had the grace to flush uncomfortably. There was no doubting first the concern and then the anger on Bruce's features as I finished my story.

"I'm going to the chapel. If this is your doing, Fern, I'm clearing out of this house in the morning and so is Melinda."

"I swear it isn't," Fern exclaimed.

"Oh, please don't take Melinda away," Charity cried. "I don't want Melinda to go. She's my friend. Please, Delphine, don't let Bruce take her away."

"Be quiet," Mrs. Jager said. "I suggest you investigate the chapel, Bruce."

"I intend to, immediately."

The next moment he had left the house.

I arose, once more in control of myself. "I'm going too. He may be in danger. Billy Cornell is out there somewere."

"I'll go with you," Mrs. Jager said.

"So will I," Fern said. "But I'll walk ahead of both of you, then Melinda will know I mean her no harm."

"Stop being silly," Mrs. Jager replied tartly. "You can't blame Melinda for thinking you did this to her. After all, you are an accomplished pianist and you've also dabbled at the organ."

"I've not been in the chapel since the last funeral," Fern said flatly. "And I'm beginning to believe Melinda made up this silly story about Vincent Seaton, minus a bride, in the chapel, because she is still enamored of him."

"Stop it," Mrs. Jager said. "I'll have no more words. Tess, bring Charity upstairs and give her that milk. She looks as if she were about to faint."

"Yes, ma'am. Thank you, ma'am." I knew the reason for her sudden politeness. Her face had turned as white as the milk, for she'd been afraid she was going to have to accompany us.

I regained some of my strength with the fresh night air and I was able to keep up with Delphine at least. Fern went on ahead, strong and fleet of foot. It was a considerable distance to the chapel and took several minutes of fast walking.

The instant I saw it, I knew no one was going to believe me. The doors were securely shut, the chapel was dark. Bruce stood at the door with Fern beside him. I stopped and watched them. Delphine approached Bruce and handed him the key.

"At least I had sense enough to bring this," she said. "Well, get it over with."

Bruce unlocked the door. He struck a match, held it high over his head and walked into the chapel. He lit another match from the first one and another and another, while he walked all the way to the altar and then back again. As he came out of the church, I braced myself.

"There's no one in there. No dummies, no lights, no organ music—just the old chapel, quiet and peaceful. There's not even a single candle in the wall brackets."

My knees shook, my mind swam and I felt myself falling slowly to the ground.

SEVEN

I opened my eyes with no awareness of where I was or what had happened. My first act was to brush aside the smelling salts which Fern held under my nose. Then I saw that Bruce was there, seated beside my bed, his fingers gently touching my wrist. Mrs. Jager stood near a window, looking most severely at me.

And then it came back and I almost cried aloud in the memory of my terror. The chapel full of wax figures, some of them effigies of the newly-dead. Candles, an organ playing, the mock wedding of the dummies—all of it rushed back into my mind and I attempted to sit up.

"Just rest," Bruce said in a quiet voice. "You're perfectly safe now. It's all over. This is your own bed, your own room. We're your friends. No harm can come to you."

His voice took on almost a monotonous quality so that it all but hypnotized me. I closed my eyes and relaxed, obedient to his commands. I felt Fern's cool hand on my fevered brow and though her touch was light and soothing, I wondered why she would show compassion since she didn't like me.

Bruce spoke again. "I want you to think back to what happened, but to do so without alarm. There is no longer anything to be frightened about. Is that clear, Melinda?"

"Yes." I opened my eyes again and glanced around the lighted room. "Yes, I know that I'm safe now. I wish to sit up."

"Good," Fern said. "I'll help you."

Her strong young arms raised me. Mrs. Jager flew to the bedside and arranged the pillows so I'd be comfortable. I discovered I could even think about the chapel without a sense of panic.

"Did I tell you exactly what happened?" I asked. "I do believe I did, but things are a bit vague—"

"You told us of the wax images set up at the altar to portray a wedding scene. You spoke of the music and the lights in the chapel," Delphine replied.

"Then we all went there and—we found nothing?" I asked.

"I'm afraid that's right," Bruce said. "There was no evidence anyone had been in the chapel."

"Do you believe me when I say again I saw what I told you about?"

Bruce said, "It could have been a dream, Melinda. Now wait—" he saw the storm arising in my eyes—"I'm not saying we don't believe you. I'm only offering possibilities."

"I've had dreams that scared me half to death," Fern said. "I used to wake us screaming my head off."

"And I too know what that is," Mrs. Jager added.

"So you see," Bruce said, "it is possible that it could have been a dream and I'll tell you why. You thought you heard organ music from the chapel before, and you saw what you believed was light through the stained-glass windows. Soon after that, you posed for me in my studio. I noticed your eyes straying to my paintings of the four people who are now dead. Vincent Seaton has been in your thoughts for days, and with good reason. Now all of these things you say you saw could have been a dream, for they were all vividly implanted in your mind."

I wriggled further upright and spoke indignantly. "I saw Billy Cornell. He threw a stone at my window to attract my attention. I went out to meet him and he was gone. I heard the music. I heard it for a considerable time and I was wide awake. I hadn't gone to sleep. To have a dream you must have gone to sleep and I swear to all of you, I had not. I did hear the organ music, see the burning candles and the wax dummies. I was close enough to have touched them. It was not a dream. Please believe me, it was no dream."

"Very well," Mrs. Jager said. "You are so insistent, I'm inclined to believe you and we shall take all measures to find out who did this. Just try not to be frightened. If someone is attempting to play a horrible joke on you, we shall find that person."

Bruce arose. "I think we'd best let you rest now. You need sleep. Later, when you're awake and refreshed, I'll talk to you again about this. Meantime, don't worry and, above all, have no fear."

"I'm feeling better now," I said. "Thank you—all of you. And, Fern, I want to apologize for my rude behavior downstairs when you attempted to comfort me."

Fern brushed it aside with a smile. "I deserved it and if you're not afraid of me, I'd like to remain with you until you drift off to sleep."

"Good idea," Bruce told his sister. "It will help both of you to become acquainted. And just to set your mind at rest, I'm going out now to make a thorough search of the estate. If Billy Cornell is anywhere on the grounds, I'll find him."

"Just one thing, Melinda," Mrs. Jager said. "The tea I'm giving in your honor is the day after tomorrow. Do you wish me to cancel it?"

"No. I may as well face up to the villagers."

"You should," Mrs. Jager agreed. "Remember, we are your staunch friends. Remember, too, it is important for those women to remain on good terms with me. I'm sure they'll accept you. Now I must go and get some rest for it is almost dawn." She and Bruce walked to the door where she paused to add, "Fern, don't talk so much that you interfere with Melinda's rest."

After the door closed behind them, Fern rearranged my pillows so that I could lie down.

"I remained because I wanted to tell you what a fool I've been to act so unkindly toward you."

I was pleased to hear Fern say this, but I was also curious as to why she was doing so. "Just why did you dislike me? Was it really because of Vincent Seaton?"

"Yes," she admitted. "I guess we were both foolish where he was concerned."

"We were," I agreed.

"I just couldn't bear it when I heard you were coming to live here. Vincent had told me, a few weeks before his death, he never wished to see me again. You see, I'd seen him with you in the village and was jealous. Especially when he told me you were his favorite girl. That if he ever married and settled down with any girl, it would be with you."

"Vincent would never settle down," I replied, "regardless of whom he married."

"I know that now," Fern said, and her smile was wistful. "However, he did have a way of making a girl feel very wonderful."

"He did, but he was a hypocrite, though undeserving of the horrible fate he met."

"I think he did deserve it," Fern said sternly. "I imagine

87

he made love to many girls and never meant a single word he said."

"Perhaps he meant it at the time he said it," I observed. "He was quite a romanticist."

"Well, I believe I've gotten over him, and do you know why?"

"Suppose you tell me," I said with a smile.

"Bruce is in love with you and tonight, downstairs, I could see that you love him also."

I could feel the color flood my face. "I didn't know it was so evident."

"It is," she said, her smile amused. "And now, I must tell you something more, something I believe will make you feel better. I believe you saw something in the chapel tonight. I believe there were candles lighting it up."

My eyes widened. "Oh, thank heaven, you do, Fern. But will you tell me what makes you say this?"

"Because when I stepped into the chapel, I thought I could smell the burned wax and the wicks."

"But Bruce said there were no candles."

"Nevertheless, I detected the odor of burning wax."

"Why didn't you tell your brother and your aunt?"

"I don't know," she said slowly. "Perhaps I didn't want you to be believed. Perhaps it was because I was still feeling resentful of your treatment of me downstairs. Perhaps I even resented the fact that I discovered you and Bruce were in love."

"Fern," I spoke quietly, "you forget, someone was playing the organ. I knew you were an accomplished piano player. I thought you were playing a horrible game on me."

"Do you still think it was I playing the organ?" she asked, her tone almost hostile.

"I don't know," I said honestly.

"Well, I'll still say I smelled wax in the chapel, but that doesn't mean I've accepted your story of the wax dummies of those five dead people or the dummies who were sitting in the pews. Frankly, it sounds too fantastic to be believed."

"I know," I replied. "I well know. And now if you'll excuse me, I think I'll try to get some sleep."

"Do you wish me to stay?"

"That won't be necessary," I replied.

"I must put out the lamps. It's one of my aunt's rules."

"I know. I'm not afraid."

Fern moved about the room quietly, extinguishing the lamps, bade me a good night and then went into the sitting room where the light there gradually faded until all was in darkness.

I did sleep, for several hours. When I awakened the slant of the sun coming in my windows told me it was late afternoon. The horror of what I'd been through came back with a rush, but not with the same impact. I could think calmly about it and I lay back against my pillows to search my mind for some reason why all of this had happened.

The wax images of those people had been works of art. They looked so real I'd been deceived. Whoever created them was an artist—and Bruce was an artist. There was another thing. Alice Townsend's portrait, as painted by Bruce, depicted her with a little half smile of her lips and her eyes. The wax face of Alice had worn an identical expression.

Bruce had been away on an emergency case, though I had no proof of it. He had reached the chapel long before the rest of us, for he'd ridden there, but I doubted he'd had time to remove all those figures, snuff the candles, take them from their holders, lock up the chapel and calmly wait for us to appear.

Someone had put on this grisly show for my benefit, but I scorned the idea of it being Bruce. I refused to consider it further and I dismissed the whole thing from my mind for the time being.

I took a leisurely bath, spending more time than usual with my toilette. At dinner time I was ready to join the others. No one had come near me, probably because they believed I was still asleep.

I surprised them by walking into the dining room just before Mrs. Jager arrived. Bruce came quickly to escort and seat me and by his beaming face I knew how glad he was to see me. I was barely settled in my chair before his aunt appeared.

"Why, Melinda," she said, her features brightening at sight of me. "How splendid to see you looking so well and at the table with us. I trust you slept soundly?"

"Yes, thank you."

"You must be ravenous, not having eaten since dinner last night." She looked up at Mrs. Linton who had entered with the maids—their trays, as usual, heavily laden with food. "See that Miss Marston is served first this evening. She hasn't eaten the entire day."

"Yes, ma'am," the housekeeper replied and motioned one of the maids over to me.

A fruit cocktail was placed on my plate and I must say the sight of it made my mouth water.

"And now, my dear," Mrs. Jager said, when everyone was served, "do you still believe you witnessed the scene you told us about in the chapel, or are you convinced it was a dream?"

I smiled. "I would swear it happened, but it sounds so bizarre, I know it is difficult for anyone to believe. Perhaps it was a dream."

I knew it was not, but I knew also that not one person at the table believed it to be a reality, or if they knew it to be so, were concealing that fact well.

"I hope I never have one like that," Charity said in her timid way. "I'd never get over it as long as I lived. I think I'd lose my mind."

Fern snickered. "Then you'd better stop eating all those sweetmeats the way you do before going to sleep. Dreams come mostly on a full stomach and from what you have in your room, you should have constant nightmares from the moment you set your head on the pillow."

Charity giggled. "I never dream and I eat anything I wish. Is it true, Bruce, what Fern just said?"

"There are medical opinions that lay claim to such a point," Bruce said. "But, in Melinda's case, remember that she's been under a great strain for some time. Her waking mind has been filled with tragedy, so it's no wonder she has frightening dreams."

I felt a tight band of pain around my heart at Bruce's words because they showed he was convinced that none of the things I had told him were true. He really believed I'd had a nightmare. I knew they were bizarre, yet I'd hoped for his trust. I recalled his manner last night. So tender, so understanding, and I had thought he knew I spoke the truth. Yet how could I blame him? There had been no evidence when we went to the chapel. Nothing but the smell of burnt wax. I looked at Fern, hoping she would speak out in my behalf and tell them what she had told me, but she was giving her entire attention to removing a mint leaf from her dish of fruit. Whether purposely or not, I didn't know.

If they had no knowledge of what had gone on in the chapel last night, then I could not blame them for their lack of belief. A long-unused private chapel occupied by wax figures, bridesmaids, a best man, a groom, organ playing—all of it seemed like a nightmare, yet I knew it wasn't. My own eyes had viewed the ghastly scene.

"Let us have no more talk of it," Mrs. Jager declared. "I wish to speak of a pleasant subject—the tea tomorrow afternoon. Everyone, I am pleased to say, has accepted. Not that it surprised me."

Charity, a sly smile on her face, said, "They know better than to cross you, Delphine."

Mrs. Jager laughed and Fern joined in. Bruce's eyes met mine and I was heartened by the tenderness and sympathy they revealed. He knew the misery I would undergo tomorrow. Also, I could see it was distasteful to him that his aunt was able to force the ladies in the village to bow to her will.

Somehow, I wondered if the tea would be the success Mrs. Jager expected it to be. I doubted strongly that the ladies would accept me. Vincent had been a most popular figure as he strode along the village streets, always removing his hat when he met a lady, regardless of her age, then bowing graciously and extending a compliment. He was like an actor, I thought, always playing a role and enjoying it to the utmost. Thinking back, I felt pity for him.

Delphine was still talking about the tea and I forced my attention back to what she was saying.

"It's to be a most lavish tea," Delphine went on. "Fern, have you arranged to loan Melinda that afternoon frock?"

"No, Aunt Delphine," Fern replied. "But I'll have Tess bring it to her room tonight."

"Good. Charity, for once you will forego your afternoon nap and appear with us. I'll expect you to be congenial and pleasant."

"Delphine, you know I'd rather not—" A look of abject misery crossed Charity's features.

"Nonsense. You cannot hide in your rooms every time a social affair takes place in this house. One day you will be mistress of Mystic Manor, and you'll be expected to grace these functions even more often than I give them. You have Melinda to help you dress and tell you what to say to the ladies."

"Yes, Delphine," Charity replied meekly.

My own distaste for the tea was equal to Charity's, though for a different reason. I felt sorry for the poor woman.

Charity's attention was given to the serving of roast beef which had just been placed on her plate. Fern looked bored and Bruce maintained a patient silence, as did I, though I was sorely tempted to give her an argument. However, I had been in this house long enough by now to know that no one argued with Mrs. Jager. She was the law. I thought to myself she was also a tyrant, yet she got her own way with such finesse that one was automatically placed at a disadvantage in attempting to defy her.

After dinner, we went, as usual, to the family drawing room and Fern once again played for us. This time, selections from Chopin and I had to admit I thoroughly enjoyed them. Yet at the same time, I couldn't help but wonder if it had been she who had played the organ. I knew of no one else in the family who did. Perhaps she had mentioned the odor of burnt wax to throw suspicion on Bruce, for he had not spoken of it, though it was quite possible he hadn't noticed it.

Tonight, to my satisfaction, Bruce managed to take his place next to me on the settee.

"I'm disappointed that so many things have happened we've been forced to cancel two sittings, Melinda. May I look forward to day after tomorrow?"

"Of course," I whispered, so as not to disturb Fern at her playing.

"Good. We mustn't neglect that portrait because I have a feeling it's going to be exceptionally good. I want to finish it as soon as possible."

I dared not look at him; I feared my eyes would reveal the thought running through my mind. Was his desire for haste because he also wished to secretly make a wax image of my head? After all, a bridegroom had been waiting in the chapel and there'd been no bride. Should that position be reserved for me, I would be the exception in that macabre group, for I'd be the only representative who was alive.

Or would I be?

Fern finished playing and Mrs. Jager arose in the customary signal that the evening was at an end. I went upstairs with Fern, for Charity had scurried ahead of us and had already reached the sanctuary of her rooms. Mrs.

Jager was supervising the locking up of the Manor, following Tess around as she checked to see that the windows were locked.

At my door, Fern said her good-night and would have continued on, but my hand lightly gripped her arm.

"Why didn't you tell your aunt and Bruce about the odor of burnt wax?" I asked of her.

"Because I'm not certain I smelled it," she replied, her manner almost glib.

"But you said——"

"Never mind what I said. If you mention it, I'll deny I said it. I believe the whole thing was the figment of your imagination. Now if you'll let go of my arm, I'll go to my rooms."

My hand dropped to my side and I watched her disappear down the corridor. What, I wondered, had happened to change her? Had she sought to gain my confidence to weaken my suspicion of her? Or was she really uncertain she had detected the odor of burnt wax? I sighed wearily and turned to enter my room when I heard footsteps behind me. Glancing over my shoulder, I saw Bruce, moving swiftly toward me.

"What is it, Melinda?" he asked. "You look very unhappy."

"I'm not," I replied. "Just confused. Good night, Bruce."

"Melinda, please——" His arms reached out and I do believe they were about to enclose me, but I moved swiftly and was in my room with the door closed behind me. I heard him speak my name softly, three times, and I pressed my cheek hard against the framework to keep from throwing the door open and going to him. I needed someone to trust, but was Bruce the one? I did not know. I could not be sure and doubt clouded my mind.

I moved over to a chair and sat down wearily, not from physical fatigue, but from mental anguish.

And once again, in my loneliness, I had the time and the opportunity to think. First of all, I told myself, my horrifying experience had not been a dream. It was as real as this room. But who was doing this to me and why? To frighten me from the estate? For what reason? Only Fern had given me to understand that my presence here was not to her liking. Bruce had declared his love for me; Mrs. Jager claimed to be my staunch ally, and Charity seemed to enjoy my company and my efforts to make her life pleasanter.

So why the motley assembly in the chapel? It represented an enormous amount of work on someone's part. Not just a few days, but months of it, for there'd been considerably more than a score of those images, each one done with extreme care and skill.

What had happened to all those figures? If they'd been in the chapel, as I knew they had, someone must have moved them. The distance couldn't have been great; there wasn't time to transport them far. When I fled the chapel, I'd rushed back to the Manor and though I'd been delayed there for the better part of half an hour, Bruce had ridden fast to the chapel only to find it locked, in darkness and empty. Could all those figures have been moved in that short time? Could all the burning candles have been snuffed and removed from their holders, including those in the chandelier in the middle of the chapel?

Yet it had been done and again the question, by whom? Bruce was the only member of the family not present at the Manor house at the time I was lured to the chapel. He was the only artist in the family. He was the first to reach the chapel and well ahead of the rest of us, for he'd ridden his horse there. If Fern had noticed the odor of burning candles, why hadn't Bruce?

Many of the answers to the mystery seemed to lie with him. Much of what I'd seen seemed to point to his guilt. I didn't want to believe this, but the facts were there. Nor could I forget he'd painted four of the people represented in the chapel and he'd attested to their deaths soon afterwards. Still, what could be his motive for frightening me— what would he have to gain?

Curiously enough, I'd believed Bruce when he told me he loved me, because I wanted to, and I still longed to hear those words of endearment on his lips once again. I wanted to feel his arms enclose me. Yet this very man who claimed my heart also put fear into it. I was frightened. I wasn't ashamed to admit it.

I jumped up to pace the room in anguish and suddenly I noticed the stack of envelopes to the dinner party on my desk. They were addressed, sealed and stamped, and needed only to be posted. I would place them downstairs the first thing in the morning so they would be taken to the village.

I put out the lamps in the sitting room and as I moved on into my bedroom, a discouraged sigh escaped me, because I'd neglected to see that the invitations had been mailed.

But when I entered my bedroom, I stood stock-still and my eyes widened in amazement, for there, placed carefully on a chaise longue, was the most beautiful mauve silk teagown I had ever seen. I picked it up and gently placed it before me as I went over to a full length mirror, which stood in one corner of the room. I smiled in pleased satisfaction as I held it against my figure.

It was, as Mrs. Jager had predicted, a perfect fit, and the fact that it was not mine affected me not in the slightest. I was too thrilled at the thought of wearing such a lovely dress. Perhaps, I thought daringly, the ladies would be so entranced with it, they would forget their animosity—at least for the afternoon. I felt greatly uplifted as I placed the frock in the closet and prepared myself for bed. Tomorrow might prove to be an exciting day, after all. I wanted to get a night's rest, for I intended to look my best.

EIGHT

The ladies, among whom was Mrs. Larkin, arrived at three —exactly twenty-two of them. They were the so-called social elite—I surmised Mrs. Jager would have little to do with the ordinary farm housewife—and they had dressed in their best for the occasion.

Fern's teagown fitted me perfectly and I minded not the least that it had been loaned me for the occasion. I took special pains with my hair, twisting it into a low looped plait and topping it with a ribbon bow of a deeper shade of mauve than the dress.

Charity was most reluctant to go downstairs, but when I explained that she would be doing me a favor, for it wasn't going to be easy for me either, she consented, though she glanced longingly at her bed as we left her boudoir. She would far rather have spent the afternoon napping. I regarded this tea party as a prelude to the affair three weeks hence and I hoped Charity would make the effort to mingle a little with the guests, though I knew it would not be easy for her. I felt a deep compassion for this timid woman.

Fern looked radiant in a Nile-green dress, with matching slippers, but when I complimented her on her appearance, her expression of thanks, while courteous, was cool.

Mrs. Jager, wearing pink, stood beside me at the entrance to the large drawing room and she greeted each lady as she entered, then introduced me. In turn, each one shook my hand and mumbled a few polite words. Some I knew, for I'd taught their children in school; others were strangers. But the manner of all of them was the same—chillingly aloof.

After the last arrival, I went over to sit beside Charity and Mrs. Jager moved to the center of the room to command the attention of the ladies. When all had ceased their chatter, she announced that Fern would honor us with a piano recital.

It was, as usual, good and at its conclusion, tea was served on small tables brought in by the maids. There were dainty, tasty sandwiches of chicken and a ham salad, all of it zesty and popular, judging from the way it disappeared. There were cupcakes, small individual pies, cookies of several kinds and, finally, an ice.

They ate heartily and I thought to myself, their husbands would undoubtedly get leftovers tonight—these ladies had made no attempt to restrain their appetites.

Of course, no self-respecting tea party really gets started until the conversation begins to hum. It did, in every section of the room where I was not. When I moved about, with Charity at my side, the conversation dwindled and died. When I offered some topics of my own, no one answered or commented. In fact, I was being snubbed. There were several times when they didn't even listen, but opened up other conversations while I was still speaking.

Charity, who had followed me about, suddenly began to sniffle. In a few moments she'd be in tears. There was no help for it. I took her elbow and led her out of the parlor and on up to her rooms.

"I don't care," she said. "If afternoon teas give them an excuse to cut you, then I don't like afternoon teas, and I hate those women. They've no right to treat you that way."

"It doesn't matter," I said soothingly. "They can't hurt me any more. I became used to it some time back. Now you can have a little nap after all. I'm sure your sister will understand."

"Are you going down there again?" Charity asked in dismay.

"It's my tea party," I said with a sigh. "Your sister would never forgive me if I didn't return. I'll see that you're awakened in time for dinner. Don't worry about me."

Charity placed a hand on my arm, timidly, and her smile was just as shy as ever. "I like you so much, Melinda. I don't know how I can ever do without you. I hope you'll never leave."

"My staying here or leaving is completely dependent on your sister. Have a nice nap."

I closed the door and went downstairs again. I could hear the chattering, eager voices all the way down the stairs. When I stepped into the room, the conversation stopped. All eyes were upon me. I merely went to one of the tables on which the sandwiches were placed. I helped myself to a plate, selected what I wished and poured myself a cup of tea, for I hadn't yet partaken of any refreshment.

I took this to an empty corner, sat down and began to eat. Until now I hadn't had an opportunity to enjoy my own party, but I intended to, despite the guests' unfriendly manner. It was to be expected, so I felt no injury.

Mrs. Jager was watching me with what I judged was not a kindly expression, and I felt unconcerned about that as well. I supposed it was because I'd brought Charity upstairs. I realized how impossible it was going to be to remain in this house much longer. The wagging tongues that made life unbearable in the village had now followed me here. Even my strong resolution not to budge until I'd found out who killed Vincent was weakening. It didn't seem to matter any more. Things would be precarious for me, but I preferred that to this polite—and sometimes not so polite—snubbing.

I finished my tea and sandwiches and seriously considered approaching one group in an effort to draw them into conversation. I was more than a little piqued, though I'd certainly known what to expect. I believed this tea party gesture to be an extremely poor idea on Mrs. Jager's part. She should have known how the guests would act toward me. Not even her importance could change their attitude regarding my guilt.

I hadn't even missed Fern until I saw her walk briskly into the room, followed by Peggy Vendeveer, the wife of the village constable. Fern walked purposefully toward me. All conversation died as the assembly realized something dramatic was about to happen. I did too, though I couldn't possibly guess what form it would take.

Fern and Mrs. Vendeveer stopped directly in front of me. Fern raised her clasped hand and then opened her fingers to allow a silver medallion to dangle from a chain. I stared at it aghast, because I knew whose it was and what it meant.

Fern said, "Is this your property, Melinda?"

I shook my head slowly and felt my courage falter as all eyes trained themselves upon me. "No, it is not. It happens to be a medallion that Vincent Seaton used to wear on his watch chain and which everyone here knows perfectly well was undoubtedly stolen from his dead body before he was found."

"Then what in the world was it doing in your room?" Fern asked coldly.

"I had no idea it was in my room, any more than I

knew Vincent's purse was in my room and which Mrs. Linton found there. Your aunt and I brought that to Constable Vendeveer's home."

"You did indeed," Mrs. Vendeveer said, with an air of authority. "It is now in my husband's possession. He has never been convinced that you killed Vincent. This medallion should help change his mind. I can certainly attest to the fact that Fern and I found it in your room."

"May I ask what you two were doing there?"

"The door was wide open," Fern said. "I happened to look in and see this medallion hanging from its chain, caught in the drawer of the sitting room table. Mrs. Vendeveer recognized it. Now that I have answered your question, please answer mine. What was this doing in your possession?"

"I don't know how the purse got into my rooms, and I don't know how this medallion got there either. I swear I did not have them. Someone who wishes me ill placed them both where they would be found, so suspicion would be cast on me for the murder of Vincent."

"I shall inform my husband that is your story," Mrs. Vendeveer said haughtily. "I presume you do not object to my turning the medallion over to him."

"I do not. It's not my property," I said, meeting her supercilious gaze. I'd known this tea party would be a failure, but I had hardly anticipated such an embarrassing crisis as this. If I fled the room, it would seem that I was admitting my guilt. Therefore, I knew I must remain and brazen it out.

"Very well," Mrs. Vendeveer said. "I, for one, do not care to remain here any longer. The tea, given for you, was an extremely generous gesture on Delphine's part, I must say, but after this"—she held the medallion aloft— "any event given in your name is not one I feel obliged to attend." She turned to Mrs. Jager. "My apologies, Delphine, but I'm sure, under the circumstances, you will not object."

There were murmurs of approval from the ladies, all of whom arose promptly. Mrs. Jager, for once, was speechless and her face flamed with embarrassment. She moved to the door, touching fingers with the departing guests and offering her apologies for what had happened.

Fern moved over to stand before the fireplace, her eyes never leaving me. There was a slight smile on her face.

"Thank you, Fern," I said, "for that remarkable display of loyalty."

"But Melinda," she said with a look of innocence I found most annoying, "it was the constable's wife who saw the medallion, not I, so I couldn't very well stop her from taking it."

Mrs. Jager waited until the door had closed behind the last guest, then walked over to Fern. Without warning, she slapped the girl across the face hard. Fern was astounded, but no more so than I. The older woman then turned to me.

"Come upstairs to my room at once, Melinda."

"Yes, Mrs. Jager." Leaving Fern to nurse her wounded pride and her smarting face, I followed Mrs. Jager from the room.

Mrs. Linton was in the reception hall. She'd witnessed the whole thing and her glare, as I passed, was one of intense anger. I pretended not to notice and continued on my way.

Mrs. Jager's door was already closed, so I tapped lightly on it and she bade me enter. Her sitting room was of an enormous size and most luxuriously furnished in very feminine white and gold French furniture of the mid-eighteenth century. Its grace and beauty were a joy to behold.

Mrs. Jager was already seated in a pink satin-upholstered chair and she motioned me to one opposite her.

"What happened this afternoon is regrettable. I know the embarrassment it must have caused you and I am sick at heart over it."

"The tea party was a mistake. But then, to begin with, I should never have come here."

"I believed it would do you some good. Perhaps it might have if Fern hadn't turned up with that bit of jewelry——"

"I didn't know it was in my room, Mrs. Jager."

"Delphine is the name my friends use. Use it!"

"Thank you. Like the purse, the medallion was placed in my room so it would be found and brought to your attention. I am not entirely a fool, Delphine. Had I been implicated in the murder of Vincent, none of his possessions would have knowingly been in my hands, though no one will believe that, of course."

"I know, my dear. And because of that, I feel it useless for you to remain here longer. You will only suffer further humiliation."

I nodded in understanding. Her words came as no surprise; I had sensed she was going to suggest my leaving. It seemed the only sensible thing to do.

"I am not sending you away in any great rush," Delphine said. "But I know when I'm utterly defeated. Now I shall see to it that you have sufficient money to help you until you have found employment."

"Thank you, Delphine, but I will accept none," I said.

"You have no choice," Delphine said. "I insist on making some arrangements. I know you have very little. You may call it a loan and repay me, if you wish."

"Under those circumstances I will accept your generous offer."

"You should go quite some distance away from here and forget this whole sorry episode in your life. Fortunately the murder did not receive a great deal of publicity, nor was there wide notoriety for you. A thousand miles from here, no one will ever have heard of the affair."

"You are probably right. I shall have to think about where to go, but I will leave soon."

"It pains me to see you go. Charity has come to love you very much and I'm sure you would have been a great help to her. Since you've been here, she's been much more cheerful. Oh my dear, what will Bruce say about this?"

"I'm sure he'll see the logic to it."

"I hope so. But he loves you."

"And I love him, though I have not told him so. Whether I do or not is of small consequence now. I could hardly marry him and remain here, and he couldn't give up his practice to go elsewhere with me and begin again. No, it's best if I just cut all ties. But one matter does worry me—the portrait. Bruce is most intent on doing it. I hate to disappoint him."

"You shan't. Bruce works quickly. Two or three days— he needs no more, and indeed, I would wish you to remain that long. Then it wouldn't seem as if I were bowing to the dictates of those petty village women."

"You're most kind. And understanding, I might add. Please don't blame Fern too much. She told me it was Mrs. Vendeveer who saw the medallion and if so, there was little she could do about it."

Delphine said thoughtfully, "I have friends in California——"

"California?" I gasped. "But that's so far away——"

"All the better. I shall send them a letter at once, asking them to intercede for you with whatever important people they know so you may find instant employment. Now why didn't I think of that before? And the journey will be good for you. It's most interesting."

"I don't know what to say. You're being too generous."

"Then it's agreed. At least let me try to make something a bit pleasant out of this disagreeable task of asking you to leave the Manor."

"How can I say no? I'll speak to Bruce the moment I see him, and find out how long he requires to get the painting to a point where he can finish it without me. And now, until dinner, I do feel the need for some rest. The strain of the afternoon has left me exhausted."

"I quite understand. May I add that through it all, your behavior was exemplary. I too intend to rest a bit. It was a disastrous afternoon."

I went slowly to my suite, suddenly aware that I would be here only a few more days. The idea didn't seem unpleasant; I had been through too much. Also, I had to admit that Mystic Manor frightened me. The misery I'd known in the village after Vincent's murder, instead of diminishing, had only heightened after my arrival here. The one sad note was the thought of leaving Bruce. It wouldn't be just a brief parting. It would, rather, be a farewell. It grieved me to realize that I had met my love, only to lose him again. I hadn't even admitted to him I loved him and it was just as well. Nor had I ever felt the touch of his lips on mine, to know the ecstasy of his closeness. That, too, would have made the parting more difficult. But I had decided I could stand no more mental anguish and so I must sacrifice my love.

What did it matter if I stayed to learn who killed Vincent? I had no means at my disposal of getting at the truth. The murderer would be found as quickly with me three thousand miles away, as right here in the village. Even if the murder was solved and I was totally cleared, I knew I couldn't live here any longer. There'd always be the breath of scandal attached to my name.

I did wonder what the reaction of the others would be when they heard the news. Fern's would be one of relief, Charity would, no doubt, break down, and Bruce—dear Bruce. . . . Despair filled me at the thought of never seeing him again.

But I was in for a surprise when Delphine entered the dining room that night for dinner, and addressed me before she sat down.

"The matter we discussed, dear Melinda, is one best kept private for the time being."

"Whatever you wish, Delphine," I said obediently.

"What matter?" Charity asked instantly.

"It does not concern you," Delphine said. "Nor anyone else at this table."

She looked around defiantly. Then she signaled and Mrs. Linton began supervising the service. There was no hint of the anger she bore me this afternoon, which surprised me. Perhaps Delphine had warned her.

As usual, after dinner we listened to Fern's piano playing and then started for our respective rooms. At the foot of the stairs, Bruce caught up with me and gently tugged at my arm.

"It's a beautiful evening," he said. "Let's take a walk. I want to talk with you."

"Very well." I was glad he'd suggested it because, despite Delphine's request, I did feel that Bruce should be told.

We went out into the moonlight-swept gardens. The air was warm and perfumed from the rose arbors. Bruce led me to a wooden bench in the midst of one formal garden and we sat down. Neither of us said anything for a few minutes. Then Bruce spoke.

"When will you be leaving the Manor?"

"You are astute, Bruce. How did you guess?"

"After what I heard about the tea party, I felt you wouldn't remain."

"That's true and your aunt was discerning enough to understand."

"Did she suggest it?"

"Yes, but it was on my mind."

"How soon will you leave?"

"Delphine agrees that it would be well if I remained long enough so that you might get my likeness on canvas. She says you work fast."

"At least I'll have your presence for a few more days. Do you know where you'll go?"

"Delphine has friends in California——"

"California!" he exploded. "What nonsense is that? Why must you go so far?"

"Bruce, I have no money. I need work. I can't very well

103

accept a loan from Delphine and then not follow her suggestions. I happen to believe she is right. The further I get away from here, the better."

"California has a wonderful climate, they tell me. I've also heard it's somewhat primitive, even in San Francisco. What will you do?"

"Teach, if I can find the work."

"Teachers should be in demand out there. Doctors as well."

"Bruce, what are you saying?"

"That I'm going with you."

I was startled by that sudden statement. "Bruce, you can't leave all this."

"All what? This is Delphine's, not mine."

"But some day it will be yours."

He smiled. "I'm not interested in acquiring anything from my aunt. And to ease your mind, Charity is her heir, though Fern and I are to supervise the estate for her. Fern can do that. She's a capable sort. All I've got is this village practice. After what's happened, I can leave that without a quiver of my conscience."

"I would not let you do that, Bruce. Perhaps later, I can return. Some day the murderer of Vincent Seaton is going to be discovered."

"What makes you believe that? No one's even looking for anybody. You're the one, as far as the whole village is concerned. If you leave, they'll be more certain than ever."

"Bruce," I said desperately, "can't you see how necessary it is for me to leave?"

"Yes. Of course I see the need for it. You're wise to go. Remaining here will only be an ever-increasing problem for you. However, I want to go with you. As your husband. Together we can face anything. That is, if you love me."

"I do, Bruce, with all my heart, but——"

He drew me into the curve of his arm. "Hush, my darling. How do you expect me to remain here and be friendly and compassionate with these stupid people who blame you for something you did not do? We'll leave here together. It will take me no more than a week to settle my affairs and arrange for another doctor to take over my practice."

"I intend to leave sooner than that. Your aunt suggested two or three days. I'm staying just long enough for you to get my likeness on canvas."

"You can't leave so soon." Bruce spoke with concern. "I'll not hear of it."

"I must. Delphine needs you here. Yes, she does," I insisted, as doubt clouded his eyes. "You yourself said Charity is to be her heir and you know that she has the mind of a child. If she and the fortune are not carefully supervised, there's no telling what will happen. Even though you believe Fern could handle it, she does not have a man's capable mind. Besides, one day she will marry and raise a family. That will take her entire time. Delphine is depending on you."

"She cannot compel me to sacrifice my happiness for Charity's sake. She can place the affairs of the estate in the hands of her attorney. He's a reputable man."

"Bruce," I said, in an effort at appeasement, "perhaps one day the murderer will be discovered, then I could return. If not, then you could come to me."

"I'm not that patient," he argued. "Melinda, do you love me?"

Our eyes met and held and in them the deep emotion we felt for one another was plainly revealed.

"You know I do, Bruce."

"Then don't say another word."

His lips closed over mine and for the first time, I knew the ecstasy of true love. All my cares and worries and fears dissolved and I was aware only of the wild beating of our hearts as he held me close. My arms moved around his neck and I wished mightily I might never have to leave this dear man's side.

Even when the kiss ended, he held me close, speaking softly and tenderly the words of love every girl wishes to hear. I lay passive in his arms, wanting this moment never to end and I wondered how I could bear being separated from him. Yet I knew I must. I was frightened here. Without realizing it, I shivered involuntarily.

"What is it, my darling?" he asked, looking down at me with alarm.

"I was just thinking of how much I'll miss you."

"That made you shiver?" His voice was chiding.

"No." Then, with honesty, I added, "I hate leaving you, but I shan't mind leaving the Manor, for, truly, though you think what happened to me a dream, it was real and, for that reason, I am afraid to remain here. I only wish I could have done more for Charity."

"Yes," he agreed. "You were good for her. The sad part about it is that one day she will have to grow up and I fear it won't be too long in the future. Then, regardless of my desires, I may never be able to get away."

I moved out of the protection of his arms to regard him with concern. "Do you mean Delphine is not well?"

"She has very high blood pressure and a none-too-strong heart. She's been bled often, but it doesn't seem to bring the pressure down. I, myself, don't believe in it. I have given her medicine that helps a little, but her condition is of such long standing that there isn't much to be done."

"Oh, Bruce, how awful. I don't know———"

"Nobody does. Only you and I. Delphine herself isn't aware of how ill she really is."

"You must not leave her. You cannot," I said. "She needs you more than ever. Bruce, remain here. I'll wait for you. I promise I'll wait, no matter how long."

"I don't know. The noble sacrifice has never appealed to me. I do love and respect my aunt, but I'm in love with you. You're my life, my future. Delphine is———"

"Hush, my darling. She's been kind to you, as you have said. If you left, I would never forgive myself for being the cause of it. I've done nothing wrong and I believe things will work out for us. We must be patient."

"We'll talk of it further," he promised, "for you haven't convinced me. Tomorrow at nine, I'll be in my studio. Say nothing of what we talked about to Delphine. Any severe shock might not be good for her. I'm an idiot. I shouldn't have burdened you with this."

I let my fingers caress his cheek. "Let me share your secret burdens. It proves your love and trust in me. Now we must go in before Delphine becomes concerned about our absence."

NINE

I prepared myself for bed and once in my nightdress, I started to brush my hair, while I reviewed the events of the day. The tea had been a fiasco, but my few moments with Bruce had more than made up for them. I was filled with the joy of love, yet there was an emptiness in me too at the thought of leaving him. We would be so far apart, yet, somehow, I felt that our love would endure, despite the distance.

Now I wished I could have been able to convince him that the episode at the chapel had really happened. I didn't blame him for believing I'd had a nightmare. What I had seen certainly seemed like the wild fancies of an overactive imagination.

Then there was the matter of the medallion—and also the purse which, too, had been the property of Vincent Seaton. There was nothing fanciful about them. They were real, seen by all and found in my suite. I marveled that Bruce didn't doubt me and I was pleased that when I'd attempted to speak of it during those precious moments in the garden with him, he had placed his fingers over my lips, silencing the words which I sought to voice, words which would have told him I was innocent and totally ignorant of how those items happened to be in my suite.

He wouldn't let me speak! The words burned into my brain as if they'd been seared there with acid. Did he know something which he had not told me? Did he really love me? Was he truly sorry that I was leaving the Manor? Or could he have been relieved that I would soon be far away and the murderer of Vincent in no danger of being uncovered?

Why had Vincent been murdered and who could have killed him? Those were the questions that now concerned me. I was the only suspect and that was because we had been overheard quarreling on the street. Could it have been a woman who had been scorned by Vincent? Or one Vincent had told he no longer cared for? Fern? Why not? If so, she could have planted those items in my room. Mrs. Linton was her staunch ally. Fern could have put the woman up to searching my baggage, knowing she would find the purse there. As for the medallion, Fern could have brought Mrs. Vendeveer upstairs on some pretext, loitered outside the door of my room so that the medallion—which she had already placed so that it hung from the drawer—caught Mrs. Vendeveer's attention.

If it wasn't a woman who had killed Vincent, who then? There had been four violent deaths prior to Vincent's, three of which had been deemed accidental and the fourth a suicide. But was that the truth? Could all four have been murders? Had Vincent uncovered some evidence and confroned the murderer with it? Or did the murderer just think Vincent knew something which was dangerous and so killed him? If so, who could that murderer be? Only one logical suspect came to mind. Bruce!

Oh, dear God, no! Let it not be Bruce! Don't let the man I love be a murderer! Just because he had painted portraits of those four people, as he was now painting mine—! *Painting mine!* Those words pinwheeled around in my head. Was I about to be murdered? Or could I save myself by leaving the Manor before the portrait was finished? I certainly had an excuse—my pride. I no longer wished to remain here. I'd been accused by Fern. I'd been humiliated at the tea party. My mind, seeking to excuse Bruce, was placing the blame for Vincent's death on her. Certainly she was a headstrong girl; certainly she had a motive. Charity had told me Fern had a gun and knew how to use it.

If the murderer was in this house, undoubtedly those figures in the chapel were placed there to make me seem mentally unbalanced. Someone knew I was telling the truth, but could glibly dismiss it by my fantastic story of the wax figures. Fern derided my story—Bruce was sympathetic. But was he really? Was his behavior a sham to cover up his evil intent? Could I love him so if he were a vicious killer? Or was he protecting Fern? There had to be an answer. Would that I could find it.

My mind turned once again to the chapel. Twice I had seen lights in there. Perhaps there were lights in there every night. Why not maintain a vigil tonight to see if I might discover a light there? If I did, I could alert Bruce or even Delphine. With proof, they could not dispute the truth of what I had told them.

But from what spot could I watch it? Certainly not the grounds, for I might be seen. The house, then. The unused third floor. I knew the chapel wasn't visible from Bruce's studio window, but there were windows on all four sides of that floor; I'd noticed them from the grounds. I could find one and watch from there. If I saw nothing tonight, there was tomorrow evening. I would be here two or three more evenings. Perhaps, in that time, I would be lucky enough to discover something that would force the members of this household to believe I had seen what I said I did.

I extinguished my lamps and settled myself in bed. I was too excited at the thought of what I was about to do, to settle down for sleep. But I closed my eyes and forced myself to relax and rest until I was assured the members of the household had not only settled down, but were deep in sleep.

I didn't believe it had been any more than fifteen minutes since I'd put out my lamp, before I heard a sound at my door.

My first impulse was to cry out and ask the identity of the intruder. Then I decided to pretend to be asleep. I was lying on my back, but my head was turned in the direction of the sitting room. However, the draperies were drawn and the room was in pitch darkness so it was that I sensed, rather than heard, someone moving toward the bedroom.

I slitted my eyes to see if I could make out anyone. I saw a faint trace of movement at the entrance of my bedroom door, then all was still. It was as if the person who entered wished to ascertain whether or not I was asleep. Satisfied, the person withdrew, for a moment later, I heard the click of the latch as the door was quietly closed.

Who could it have been? I wondered. I had no idea. Nor could I imagine why that person had invaded my suite. Was it to ascertain I was asleep so that he—or she—could make another visit to the chapel? My eyes widened at the thought and, without a moment's hesitation, I slipped out of bed, got into my slippers, placed my cloak over my shoulders and moved silently over to a window overlooking the front of the estate. There was a moon and I had a clear view of the grounds, sweeping right down to the silver sheen of the Hudson, far below. Nothing moved, there was no stirring of branches or shrubbery, not even a night sound to disturb the quiet.

I was completely alert now and I knew that if I were to watch for a light in the chapel, there was no time to lose.

But something warned me to take precautions to keep the fact that I'd left the room a secret.

Working silently, but swiftly, I seized a heavy coat and a winter blanket from the closet, rolled them into something resembling a human form and placed it under the bedcovers. A little prodding here and stretching there and I had a rather good likeness of a body deep in sleep. I moved swiftly to my bureau, silently opened a drawer and took from it a hairpiece which I used when I dressed my hair for special occasions. I pressed the pillow down, placed the hairpiece so that, though the covers concealed what was supposed to be my face, the hair spilled over them. The effect was eerily real.

I couldn't risk taking a lamp or even a candle with me, but I did know this second floor well enough to find the stairway to the unused third floor, which was formerly the servants' quarters, without stumbling over anything. Up there I'd be a total stranger except in the room Bruce used as a studio, but I was determined to carry out this idea of mine even if there was some risk of discovery involved. After all, no one could really blame me for trying to prove my bizarre tale had some truth in it.

I listened at the door and heard nothing, so I opened it and stood just outside my rooms for two or three minutes, hardly daring to breathe, listening again. I could see no streaks of light beneath any of the doors. I judged it must be somewhere around one in the morning and knew, with the exception of one member, the household was asleep.

After closing the door to my room, I made my way down the corridor. I found the stairway and carefully placed my weight on each step, lest they creak. It was fortunate for me that Mrs. Linton occupied one of the smaller suites on the second floor, for had she lived up here I might have feared to risk this.

The third floor corridor was narrow and very dark. I had to move by sense of touch, my hands feeling along the walls until they encountered a door frame. Then I could press an ear against the door to listen. If I heard no sound, I would open the door. Fortunately, once I did, the moonlight that still swept the estate illuminated the room to a remarkable extent, since my eyes were so accustomed now to darkness. I passed by the open door of the studio, for its windows faced in the wrong direction.

All this had to be done quietly and slowly. I had no idea

if those people below were light sleepers. I thought that Charity should be, for she slept half the day and certainly never exerted herself in any way to become tired.

I found a room, finally, from the window of which I could look out over the trees, or between them. At any rate, I could see the reflection of the moonlight on the stained-glass windows of the chapel, even though it was so far away.

I wished then that the moon would retire behind clouds so that I might discover if there was even faint light in the chapel. I stood there, not daring to move for fear of disturbing those below. It wasn't cold in this musty-smelling, long-unused room, but my eerie surroundings had a tendency to chill me.

I remained there until I grew so weary I started to sway from fatigue and my eyelids began to droop. Now and then the moon did go behind a cloud and I did have an opportunity to see if the chapel windows were dark. They always were. I began to get the idea that whoever had slipped into my room to make sure I was asleep had something besides visiting the chapel in mind.

I left the room reluctantly, closed the door and made my silent way to the second floor, even going to the top of the staircase and looking down into the reception hall in an attempt to make certain no one was abroad.

The silence of the house seemed to set my nerves on edge. Each creak or groan of ancient timber had the ability to make my flesh crawl, for I felt as if it were watching me. It was a foolish thought, yet it persisted and suddenly, a strange feeling that something dire was about to happen here pervaded me.

I reached my own rooms and when I shut the door behind me, I felt much easier. The night had been a complete waste and I feared I'd not be a very good subject for a portrait in the morning when I appeared at Bruce's studio, for I'd have deep circles under my eyes from lack of sleep.

However, I vowed I'd do the same thing tomorrow night, even to rolling up the blankets so it would look as if I were in bed and fast asleep. I stepped into the bedroom and looked with some amusement and mild satisfaction at the shape under the bedcovers. It would have deceived me, I felt sure.

I took off the cloak, placed it over the back of a chair

and started to draw down the bedcovers to remove the rolled-up blanket and coat beneath it. But something seemed to be holding the covers back. Puzzled, I pulled at them impatiently and it was then I realized they seemed to be pinned down.

I bent over the bed and let my hands explore the area beyond which the covers would not move. An exclamation of horror escaped my lips as my fingers touched the object that kept the bedclothes from moving. It was a long-bladed knife which had been driven through them and into the clumsy facsimile of my body.

For a moment, my senses reeled and I clutched at the bedpost to steady myself, for, though I longed for merciful unconsciousness to envelop me, I dared not allow myself to swoon. The murderer might return.

Summoning my courage, I took a few deep breaths to steady myself and reached over to where the knife handle protruded from the bed. I pulled it free and in the dim light of the room, its blade shimmered. It was at least ten inches long and probably as sharp as a razor's edge.

I knew now the intruder had entered my room, not to make certain I was asleep so that he might go to the chapel, but to make certain I was vulnerable to attack. His only motive for leaving the room was to visit the kitchen and procure this knife.

With a cry of anguish, I dropped the knife onto the bed and ran, screaming, from the suite. In the corridor, I continued my cries until doors started to open, and lamps and candles appeared in the hands of Delphine, Fern, Bruce and Mrs. Linton.

Bruce placed his lamp on a table in the corridor. He was wearing a dressing gown, but beneath it his trousers and shirt were visible. Obviously, he had not yet retired.

Fern and Delphine had donned lacy negligees and Mrs. Linton's ample figure was covered by a voluminous wrapper. Her hair, again tightly braided, gave her a ludicrous appearance.

Bruce came to me at once and his arms enveloped me. "What is it, my dear? Another nightmare?"

"No, no, no," I replied, my voice tight with fear. "Not a nightmare. It was real. Someone tried to kill me."

"What sort of nonsense is she speaking now?" Fern asked, her features cynical.

"It's not nonsense," I exclaimed. "I left my room for a

while and prepared a form in my bed to look like me. While I was gone, someone came in and drove a knife through it."

"I don't understand, Melinda. It really doesn't make much sense," Bruce said, his features sorely perplexed. "And why did you fix up your bed that way?"

"I went upstairs to observe the chapel from a window and I didn't want anyone to know I was absent from my room. You see, someone entered it after I had retired. I thought that person was going to the chapel and wanted to make certain I was sleeping. I wanted to see if there would be any light shining through the windows."

"And was there?" Fern asked.

"No," I replied, my eyes beseeching her to believe me. She gave a little laugh. "You are a silly young woman."

"Stop it, Fern," Bruce replied, his tone angry. "If you can't be civil to Melinda, then go back to your room." His voice softened. "Where is the knife?"

"I dropped it on my bed." I looked around and further panic assailed me. "Where's Charity? Why isn't she here?"

"I gave her a sleeping draught," Delphine said. "She was quite upset over what happened this afternoon."

"But I didn't tell her about it," I said.

"I did," Delphine replied. "I've made inquiries of everyone, including the outside help, to see if there have been any strangers seen on the premises, someone who might have placed Vincent's possessions in your room. I'm sorry to say my inquiries brought no result."

"I saw Billy Cornell," I said.

"No one else did, my dear," Delphine said, her smile sympathetic.

I nodded. "That's why I wanted to see a light in the chapel tonight. If I had, I'd have gone to you at once so I could prove I wasn't having nightmares."

"I think you've just had another," Fern retorted, her glance at Bruce defiant. "First, you see wax dummies of dead people. When we refused to believe that story, you resort to another even more dramatic——saying someone attempted to murder you."

"But it's the truth," I exclaimed. "The knife is on the bed."

"Let us go in and see it," Delphine said and proceeded to enter the sitting room. Bruce and I followed and I felt the comforting protection of his arm. Fern, I presumed, was behind us.

Bruce left my side to approach the bed. Delphine, holding the lamp aloft, exclaimed in dismay as the cold steel of the blade reflected the ray of light. Bruce exclaimed aloud as he picked it up. Fern regarded it, still seemingly unimpressed.

"I wish someone would look in on Charity," I said. "Perhaps, whoever tried to murder me might harm her."

"Good Lord," Bruce said in sudden panic. Still holding the knife, he led the way from the room.

Charity's suite was halfway down the corridor. I prayed the door would be unlocked and sighed in relief as it opened when Bruce turned the knob. He motioned for silence and we followed him into Charity's bedroom. She was sound asleep, her breathing regular. She did look like a lovely, helpless child, with her head on the pillows and her hands clutching the covers, as if for protection.

"She's all right," Bruce whispered.

In the hall again, Mrs. Linton asked permission to return to her rooms. Delphine nodded.

Bruce said, "Well, we now have definite evidence that someone either in this house, or someone who has invaded these premises, tried to murder Melinda."

"Don't you think you're jumping at conclusions?" Fern asked.

"Whatever do you mean?" Delphine asked, her tone irritable.

"Why couldn't Melinda have stabbed the knife down through the covers and the rolled-up blankets just to convince us someone has been trying to harm her?"

"Fern!" Delphine exclaimed, her tone shocked.

"I've been very patient with you, Fern," Bruce said coldly, "because you're my sister. But you're far from likeable and I'm disgusted with the way you've treated Melinda. I happen to love her, I intend to ask her to marry me. So from now on, be careful of what you say."

"Why must you be so filled with suspicion and hate?" Delphine asked tartly.

"I'm not," Fern replied. "I don't like mysteries. I don't like murder. Neither do I like being accused of having attempted to murder Melinda, who happens to be a guest in this house."

"But I haven't accused you," I exclaimed.

"Can you say you haven't suspected me of having

murdered Vincent? Go on," she exclaimed heatedly. "Can you honestly say it?"

I lowered my eyes, unable to meet her gaze.

Her voice was triumphant as she said, "There, you see. She suspects us all. And you, Aunt Delphine, have befriended her. How do you feel about her now?"

"I feel Melinda has been through a great deal," Delphine said, her voice kind. "Perhaps I can't blame her for suspecting us when she claims innocence as to Vincent's effects, which were found in her room."

"That fact is what makes it so difficult for me to believe in her innocence," Fern said flatly. "I feel no personal animosity toward Melinda. I did, at first. Now I resent her because she suspects us. I don't like being suspected of murder."

"No one does," I replied quietly. "Believe me, I know."

"Then stop suspecting me," Fern cried out. "I'm innocent of Vincent's murder. I loved him. I thought I was over it, but when I saw that medallion hanging from the drawer in your room, I suffered at his loss, all over again."

"That will do," Delphine said tersely. "I'm glad that blackguard's dead. He was no good to himself or to anyone and it sickened me to see what a fool you made of yourself over him."

"Oh!" Fern exclaimed, her voice shocked at Delphine's words. A sob escaped her and, much to my surprise, she burst into tears.

"Fern, I'm sorry," I exclaimed, touched by her sudden display of emotion. "I am confused, I admit it. I have thought of the possibility that you might have murdered Vincent and, in doing so, I've been as unfair to you as the villagers have been to me. But I shan't be here much longer, so you need feel no further animosity toward me."

"You're going away?" she asked, her surprise so great that her tears miraculously stopped.

"To California," I said. "I'm remaining only long enough so that Bruce can complete enough of the portrait that he can finish it without me. I shan't be here more than a day or two at the most."

"Oh, dear," Delphine sighed. "I asked you not to speak of it. Though I know you've already told Bruce."

"I have," I admitted. "And I see no reason for secrecy."

"There is none," Delphine admitted, "except that Charity will be badly affected by your leaving."

"I'm sure you can find someone to take my place," I said. "However, I shan't mention it to her, though I think it's more unkind not to."

"I think the most important thing at the moment is for Melinda to get some rest," Bruce said. "I'm going to check the house to make certain no one got in."

"Please do, Bruce," Delphine said. "I think we should all try to get some rest out of what remains of the night."

"Would you like another room?" Bruce asked. "After what almost happened in there——"

"No," I replied. "I'll lock my door."

"First," he said, "I'll check your rooms. And if one thing more happens to Melinda, I shall leave with her."

"Bruce," Delphine exclaimed, "you wouldn't."

"I would and I will," he asserted firmly. He placed the knife on the table, picked up a lamp and went into my suite. I remained in the corridor with Delphine. Fern regarded me quietly, looked as if she were about to say something, then, still holding her candelabrum, turned to return to her rooms.

Bruce came out of my suite shortly and nodded that all was well. "I believe you'll be troubled with no more intruders. Be sure to lock your door."

"I shall indeed," I assured him. "Good night, Bruce. And, Delphine, I'm sorry I had to disturb the household."

She nodded understandingly. "I hope there'll be no further cause for it. I just wish I knew who could have done such a thing. Believe me, Melinda, I feel certain you wouldn't resort to such chicanery."

"Be assured, Aunt Delphine, she wouldn't," Bruce replied, saving me the trouble of a reply. "Go into your room, Melinda. I wish to hear your lock turn before I go downstairs."

I did as I was bade and was grateful he had seen fit to light the lamps in my suite. Despite Delphine's rule regarding lighted lamps, I was determined to let mine burn. The thought of remaining in this suite in darkness was too much for me to contemplate. Except for the fact that I would be separated from Bruce, I found myself looking forward to leaving the Manor. In the few days I'd been here, I'd been through enough unpleasantness to last me the remainder of my life.

And as for Bruce, after the way he had defended me, how could I suspect him of any wrongdoing?

TEN

Bruce refused to let me talk about the events of the night before, or any of the other grim adventures I'd undergone at Mystic Manor.

"I want you to think of California and the day I'll follow you out there. Of when I step off the train, and the day very soon after that when we'll be married. You have a sensitive face and what you are thinking shows."

"I'll do my best," I promised. "I won't guarantee the result, however. Too much has happened—I can't get it all out of my mind."

He began talking of his days in college, of his efforts to get a practice started in the village before the old doctor died and no one trusted the new and young physician. He told anecdotes and he laughed heartily at them himself, all to put me at ease. Finally I could feel the apprehension and care leave me and I began to relax.

"Now," he said, "I can go to work on the expression, the eyes, mouth—keep your mind clear. I have to work fast."

He kept at it for two hours, until I could bear no more and then he helped me into a more comfortable chair, for I was so stiff from posing I could hardly move.

"It's going to be great," he exulted. "I can tell already. You're an excellent subject."

"Have you painted your sister or your Aunt Delphine?"

He laughed good-naturedly. "I painted Delphine two or three times and destroyed all but one canvas. Even that one I'd never allow anyone to hang. Delphine poses like the Queen Mother of some mighty empire. I couldn't get her to unbend no matter how hard I tried."

"Fern would make a fine subject," I said.

"Fern has resolutely and flatly refused to pose for me. Won't even let me do a sketch. She says she doesn't want to see herself as others see her. Perhaps she's wise, for I fear she'd not like what she saw. Charity now—she posed and it came out in a most interesting fashion."

"I know. May I see it again?"

He went to a corner of the room where countless canvases were placed facing the wall. He found the one he wanted, returned with it and propped it against the chair in which he'd been sitting. It was a rather amazing portrait. Perhaps he'd flattered Charity a little. Certainly in the way of cheek color he had, for Charity went out so rarely she usually looked very pale. But it was the expression around the eyes and mouth that interested me. And I was impressed once again with his skill. He had captured very well her fragile features, timid eyes and the petulant, childish expression around the mouth. I was glad it was just a head portrait, for Bruce was so honest he'd have painted her plumpness and the body just didn't go with the face.

"It's very good," I said.

"Charity has never seen it that I know of. I thought with that childlike attitude of hers, she'd be too curious to resist, but there is a womanly quality in her that occasionally is revealed and the womanly Charity would abhor the childish one. I'm very likely being silly about the whole thing, but that's how I feel."

"Bruce, please may I speak of last night——?"

"No," he said in a kindly voice. "Not until the sitting is finished for the day. Back on the throne, your majesty. There's a tilt to your nose I find difficult to get. Perhaps I'll just paint in a small snub nose and let it go at that."

"Don't you dare," I warned him with a smile. I was at ease from the start of the second session. This was a long one because I insisted it be, so we could get as much done as possible. Finally, Bruce gave up.

"If you're not all tired out, or frozen into that pose, I'm worn out from standing in front of the canvas. We've accomplished a great deal today."

"May I see it?"

"It's well enough along now so that you can tell how it will be when finished. Come—and I hope it meets with your approval."

I was astounded with the likeness Bruce had portrayed of me, even though it was not yet completed. There were highlights in my hair and eyes and he'd molded my features softly, with the merest smile about my mouth.

"There is nothing I can say other than that I am deeply pleased."

"Thank you. I only hope I've done you justice."

He draped the canvas with a cloth, turned to me and led me over to a settee which graced one corner of the room. "You wanted to talk, darling. We have privacy here. I know there's something on your mind, as well there might be, and I thank you for forgetting it while I painted you."

"You made it possible with your very amusing stories." My face sobered. "But you're right, Bruce. I'm very concerned about last night. I've convinced myself that the effects belonging to Vincent were placed in my room by an outsider."

"Was it difficult to convince yourself of that?" Bruce asked soberly.

My smile was apologetic. "You're thinking of Fern's outburst. That did start me thinking and I realized it was wrong of me to suspect the members of this household without evidence. For I was placing all of you in the same position I'd been placed in."

"Then whom do you suspect?"

"Billy Cornell," I said. "When I first arrived here, Charity told me she was choked once and her clothes were slashed twice with a knife."

Bruce looked thoughtful. "I never heard of it."

"Perhaps she was too terrified to mention it."

"It's possible, though I wish she had. And it's quite possible it was Billy. Or maybe Charity dreamed it up in an effort to build herself up. As for Billy, I've thought of him, naturally. He's not very intelligent. In fact, he's all but moronic. I doubt he knows the difference between right and wrong, between lying or telling the truth. He loves the darkness, abhors the daylight, and people frighten him."

"Would you think him capable of filling the chapel with wax images?"

"Perhaps, but not of creating them, not of setting them to simulate a wedding, not in duplicating the faces of five dead persons."

"If the effigies were provided, do you think he might have been able to create the setting?"

"No! He lacks the intelligence and the imagination."

"Could he possibly play the organ?"

"Absolutely not."

"Suppose," I said, "he came to the house last night with this knife, with orders to kill me. Could he do that?"

Bruce nodded slowly. "Yes . . . yes, he can understand simple orders and follow them."

"Do you think he's capable of killing someone?"

"As I said, Billy can't distinguish between right and wrong. If he were told, for example, that you were evil and

119

the world would be better off rid of you, then he'd cheerfully obey an order to kill you. Or me, or anyone else for that matter."

"Billy told lies about me and the death of Vincent, and I don't know why. I've seen him around this estate twice—where he does not belong. I honestly believe he is the person who tried to strangle me that night along the path, and it's more than possible he used the knife last night."

"I've tried to find him so I could see if his face is scratched by your nails," Bruce said, "but Billy has remained out of sight ever since that happened. Therefore, it's possible he is scratched and doesn't dare show himself. As for last night—the nature of the act itself seems to indicate Billy, and I'll tell you why. If I, for instance, had slipped into your room with the knife, I doubt I would have been deceived by the bulk under the bedcovers. But even if I had, I should have known the instant the knife descended that I'd been tricked. Therefore, I should have withdrawn the knife and gone away quietly, leaving the slash marks in the blanket and covers to be a fresh mystery."

"Billy, not being of normal intelligence, used the knife and then ran away in a panic," I said. "Is that what you're driving at, Bruce?"

"Precisely. So—I'm going to see if I can hunt him down."

"Another thing. Is there any way to enter and leave this house without using the doors? Or even the windows?"

He gave me a most searching look. "Now what made you think of that?"

"The doors were bolted from inside last night, the windows were all closed and locked from inside. Delphine saw to that. If it was Billy, he had to have a way to come and go. Is there a secret way in and out?"

He nodded. "Yes. Delphine knows of it and so do I, but I don't believe anyone else does. It's a short tunnel that runs from the wine cellar in the basement to a root cellar out behind the house. We don't know when it was built, nor why, but it's scores of years old and I suspect the root cellar was once a hiding place for smuggled goods brought by one of our ancestors. The history of the family is not all it should be. I found the tunnel by accident when I was a little boy."

"Could we look at it?" I asked. "Now—at once?"

"I see no reason why not. Come along. By this time Fern is getting ready for dinner, Delphine is doing the same and Charity is sound asleep in one of her afternoon naps, so I doubt we'll be disturbed."

Bruce led me to a narrow door in a short hallway between the dining room and the rear of the entrance hall. He opened the door and went down the steep stairs first. I followed him. It was quite dark here, not with the blackness of night, but the grayness of dusk. At the bottom of the steps, he took my hand and we walked quickly to a very heavy, iron-barred door.

"Behold," Bruce said, "the wine cellar, its contents once so precious one of the former owners converted it into a veritable prison. The door hasn't been locked in fifty or more years."

It opened easily and quietly, I noticed, and we entered the dusty, cobweb-hung, musty wine cellar with its ancient racks and old barrels still smelling acridly of wine produced decades ago.

There were candles on a small table and Bruce lit two of them, handed me one. "See the tall, ceiling-high rack? The door lies behind that." He seized the rack and tugged. It opened smoothly. Behind it, blending with the dirt wall, was a cleverly constructed door which also swung easily.

Now it was necessary to bend almost double but, thank heaven, it wasn't necessary to crawl. The tunnel seemed airless and for a moment I thought the flames of our candles were going out, but some fresh air must have seeped in somehow for the flames grew bright again.

I said, "Bruce—look about you."

He moved the candle back and forth. "I see nothing."

"Quite correct. The wine cellar—at least the sides of it— were heavily hung with cobwebs. If this tunnel hadn't been used in many years, it would be almost closed by webs, but there are none."

"So I see—now that you call my attention to it," Bruce said. "I wonder if we've stumbled onto something here. Look down at your feet. The earth is hard packed, as if there's been some traffic over it lately."

"Could we," I asked nervously, "get out of here quickly?"

"Of course." He continued to lead me along the tunnel and after another dozen yards we came to a door, made of wood, thick and stout.

This opened into a root cellar so low we were compelled to go down on our knees to get to the slanting cellar doors. Bruce pushed them up and fresh air and late afternoon sunlight greeted us. Bruce helped pull me out and we stood looking down into the root cellar.

It was being used and likely had been right along. There were potatoes, turnips, carrots, and several other vegetables properly arranged so they'd keep for winter.

"Mrs. Linton would use this root cellar," I commented.

"True, but you don't actually suspect her, do you?"

"She could have told someone of the existence of the tunnel. If she crept into this cellar often enough, she likely found it."

Bruce nodded. He closed the slanting doors and turned around. The path to the chapel passed close by. I looked in the direction of the house, but I was unable to see any part of it except the very rooftop, for the trees were well grown around this cellar.

"It would not be difficult to use this passage secretly," I said.

"I agree. We do seem to be making progress. Now if we could only find Billy."

I turned the watch pinned to my dress face out and gasped. "We'll be late for dinner if we don't hurry."

"Melinda," Bruce's hand on my arm stayed me, "please don't mention to my aunt that I revealed the secret passage to you. I want to find Billy and have a talk with him before we speak to anyone in the family."

I agreed and we returned by way of the formal gardens, though I paused long enough to brush the dirt off my dress and shoes. I went directly to my suite and changed my dress, because the trip through the tunnel had soiled the one I'd worn.

As I made myself ready, I thought that at least I was making some progress in an attempt to solve the mystery. I knew now that Billy Cornell could have come and gone from the Manor house with ease, which solved many problems in my mind, for I was loath to suspect any member of the family.

Certainly someone guided Billy's movements and had provided the grisly setting of the wedding in wax, but it was Billy who'd carried out the schemes of violence. I thought of Mrs. Linton. Could it be that she had entered into a conspiracy with someone in the village? Or was she, somehow, involved?

During dinner, there was no mention of what had transpired during the night, since it had been decided that Charity not know of it, nor of my departure. Therefore, when she suddenly burst into tears, just as dessert was being served, I was amazed, but even more so at her outburst.

"You can't send Melinda away," she sobbed, directing her words to her sister. "I won't stand for it. I need her. I've never been happy before and Melinda keeps me cheerful."

"You're not cheerful now, Charity," I said chidingly.

"That's because you're going to leave the Manor."

"I'll write to you," I promised in an effort to placate her.

"If you send her away, Delphine," Charity went on, "I'll never speak to you again, or come out of my room or even eat another bite. And don't you laugh, Fern. I mean it. I'll starve myself to death. I can't do without Melinda and I won't, even if I have to go away with her myself."

"Charity, please." I placed a comforting hand on her shoulder. "Don't upset yourself this way. I'm sure that one day we'll see each other again. You wouldn't want to leave the Manor any more than you'd want me to stay here and be treated unkindly by the villagers, would you now?"

"I would, yes, I would. If you go, you won't ever come back. Please don't go, Melinda. Oh, please—you don't ever have to leave the estate. I never do. I'll be frightened when you go. You give me courage."

"Who told you Melinda was going?" Delphine asked, her voice stern.

Charity let out a loud wail, dabbed at her eyes with her napkin, then jumped up and ran from the room. I began to arise to follow her, but Delphine motioned me back into my chair.

"Let her cry it out. She can't be babied all her life. I can see I've made a bad mistake protecting her. I believe, Bruce, when Melinda leaves, I'll place Charity in your care. Perhaps you can do something with her."

"I fear it's a little too late," he said dryly. "The damage has been done. She's too old to change now and she does need someone with her. I'd hoped Melinda might be able to help her, but even with Melinda here, she sleeps the afternoons away."

Delphine sighed. "I fear you're right."

"What she needs," Fern said matter-of-factly, "is to have her face slapped good and hard."

Delphine gave her a curt look, but somehow, thinking of last night, I couldn't blame Fern.

Bruce made no attempt to hide his smile. "I can't see that the slap you got did you much good."

"Perhaps you forget that I cried last night," Fern said spitefully. "But I shan't do so again. I'm sick and tired of all the trouble and confusion we've had since Melinda came here. I'm sick and tired of Mystic Manor."

"Please leave the table, Fern," Delphine said. "I've had all of your bad manners I intend to take."

"I believe, Aunt Delphine," Fern said and her voice was as cold as her aunt's, "I shall leave the Manor, move to New York City and seek employment there."

"An excellent idea," Bruce approved. "You might learn consideration for other people's feelings."

"Really, Bruce, you're insufferable too," Fern said and, slamming her napkin on the table, fled the room.

"Oh, dear," Delphine's sigh was weary. "I suppose I should go up and attempt to pacify Charity."

"Do you wish me to do so?" I asked, also feeling distressed at the turbulent emotions which had swept around the table.

Her smile was grateful as she said, "No, my dear. I can talk with her."

"When you do," Bruce said, "you might question her as to how she discovered Melinda's plans to leave. I was of the opinion we agreed she was not to know them. At least, not until just before Melinda left."

"I'd have preferred she not have known until after Melinda was gone," Delphine said. "I don't believe Fern, disagreeable as she is with Charity, would have betrayed us. I suspect Tess. I saw her come out of Charity's room before dinner. I swear I shall be forced to discharge that woman one of these days." Her eyes regarded me questioningly. "Melinda, have you made up your mind when you'll leave?"

I glanced at Bruce. "It's up to your nephew, Delphine. The portrait is progressing well, but only he knows when it will be finished."

"Day after tomorrow," Bruce said. "I insist she stay until then."

"Very well. I have already written my California friends and now I shall write again telling them when you leave here. When you are well along your journey, Melinda, it would be wise to send them a telegram, informing them of the precise time of your arrival so they may be on hand to meet you."

"I'll be sure to remember that," I said. "Tomorrow I will pack what I can take with me and place the rest in my trunk for later shipment."

"Well, that's settled," Delphine said with a sigh of relief. "Now we must get Charity accustomed to the idea. Tonight we must forego our pleasant relaxation in the parlor. I'll go to Charity now and comfort her if I can."

Delphine walked serenely out of the room and only Bruce and I were left at the table. He poured more coffee from the heavy silver service. I added cream and sugar, stirred the coffee slowly.

"I'm riding into the village now to see if I can find Billy. There are two house calls I have to make as well. Do you wish to come with me?"

"I believe I'll be safe here now that I'm going away. I'm hoping those attacks upon me could have been only to drive me from Mystic Manor and whoever directed them must now be satisfied."

"Don't rely on that theory too much. I'll return as quickly as possible. One thing I will do, however, is block the tunnel door leading into the wine cellar so if Billy is hidden hereabouts, he won't be able to get into the Manor that way."

"I'll feel safer if you do that," I said. "Bruce, I've been thinking about your story of the smugglers. They could have brought contraband up the river with little trouble and unloaded it by night. The tunnel and the hiding place now used as a root cellar would have been fine to conceal the smuggled goods, but the space is so limited. As I see it, smugglers successful enough to build a house like this must have done a very large trade. Therefore, they must have had at least one more hiding place and a large one. What do you think of that idea?"

"Brilliant, but what point are you trying to make?"

"I believe those wax images are hidden there. Or are you still of the opinion it was a nightmare of mine?"

"After the incident of the knife, I believe everything you've told me. And as for those wedding images in wax—

plus the congregation—they'd take up a great deal of space. We'll do our best to find them, but now I must hasten to the village."

"I shall listen for your return," I told him. "The house feels more secure with you here."

"Thank you, my darling." He arose, bent down and kissed me. "Oh—did I forget to ask you to marry me?"

I smiled. "I suspected such might be your intention."

"You suspect right," he replied. "And don't you forget it. Not even in far-off California."

"I shan't," I assured him.

He drew back my chair and I arose and accompanied him to the door. He already had a horse saddled and waiting. I remained on the porch until he had ridden out of sight. Then I turned back with a slight shudder. For some reason, the lengthening evening shadows had a most depressing effect on me ever since I'd come to the Manor. I hated the oncoming of night.

I found Delphine descending the main staircase, her face clouded with perplexity.

"Charity refused to allow me to enter her rooms," she said. "I fear she might become ill, she's so upset over your leaving."

"Let me try to talk to her," I suggested.

"I wish you would, my dear." She raised a hand and gently massaged her forehead. "I am tired. And these things upset me so. I've a headache——"

"Please lie down," I begged, remembering what Bruce had told me about her health. "I feel I've brought so much of this trouble to your door, Delphine. Perhaps I can straighten out Charity. I'll do my best with her."

"Thank you. I believe I shall retire. Oh no"—she quickly rejected the offer of my arm—"I'm quite all right. Good heavens, girl, I'm not yet feeble."

We walked up the stairs together and I was rather alarmed at her appearance. There was too much color in her face and she wheezed considerably during the stair climb. At the corridor, she touched her cheek to mine in a gesture of gratitude.

"Come see me before you go to bed, Melinda. I shall tell you about these friends of mine into whose care I am entrusting you. They are delightful people."

"Thank you. I won't fail."

126

I waited while she entered her suite of rooms and then I walked down the corridor toward Charity's, wondering what I could say to pacify her.

ELEVEN

Once I identified myself by calling through the door, Charity admitted me. Her cheeks were tear-stained, her eyes red from weeping. I put my arm about her waist and led her to the yellow settee where we sat down side by side.

"I'll try not to be away for very long," I explained, "and I'll write to you often, all about the long train journey. I'll keep you informed about what it's like, what I see. Perhaps, one day, we can both take the trip together."

She shook her head in negative fashion. "I don't want to leave the Manor. I hate my sister for making you go away, Melinda. She has no right to. I'll never see you again."

"Charity, I'm leaving because I want to. I find it impossible to remain here where the women in the village regard me as a murderess. It's embarrassing for your sister, but for me, it's even worse."

"What if they don't ever find out who killed that old Vincent Seaton?"

"They will. One day they'll find out, then my name will be cleared and I'll be able to come back."

"In a month or two?" she asked hopefully.

"It may be a little longer than that," I said, keeping my voice cheerful.

"Fern did this. She's the one made my sister send you away. I hate her."

"You're wrong, Charity. Fern had nothing to do with it. Don't hate her. Be kind to her. She's a very lonely person."

"She wasn't lonely when she had Vincent Seaton. Oh yes, I know. He came here to see her. He was after her money, but she hasn't got any. He didn't know that, but when he found out, he didn't come back any more. Vincent wanted money. He didn't love any woman except you."

"That's all in the past," I said. "I don't want to talk about it. Now I'm going to spend the evening packing my things. Would you like to keep me company?"

She arose abruptly. "I don't think so. It will only make me sad. I'm very tired. I always get tired when I'm upset.

But thank you for coming to see me. I wouldn't let anyone else in. I'm going to lock the door and go to bed. I won't talk to Delphine and I won't see Fern for any reason. I don't even want to see Bruce and he's always been kind to me."

"Very well," I said, rising. "I'm going to retire soon also. Good night, Charity."

She embraced me and began to sniffle again, this woman with the instincts of a child. I wondered, had I been able to remain here, if I might have been able to help her. More than anything else, she needed to get out among people, acquire confidence and grow up. It would be a painful process at her age, but it had never seemed to me that she was mentally deficient, merely mentally asleep.

I made my way to my own rooms and there I began to organize my things for packing. On a journey like this, even with much of my possessions to be shipped by express, I couldn't take everything. As I worked, my interest in the packing grew less and less, for my mind was going around in circles concerned with the probable existence of the smugglers' hiding place Bruce and I had discussed.

Once again I reasoned that the dummies in the church had been removed very quickly, so their hiding place must be close by the chapel. Perhaps that's where the original smugglers' place was located. The whole area around the chapel was uncultivated and grown rather wild. Brush, trees, rocks, mounds of earth, all could hide an entrance.

If I could find such a hiding place, come across the wax images there, then my story would be accepted and quite possibly those in authority would conclude that this bizarre situation must have something to do with the murder of Vincent—possibly of four other persons whose deaths were not even listed as murder. There was even a chance the true killer would be found and then I'd not have to go away at all.

I could stay here and be with Bruce. I could try to help Charity and in some measure repay Delphine for all she had done and wanted to do for me.

Finding the hiding place of the wax dummies was the most important thing in my life at this moment. I ceased worrying about getting ready for the journey. I changed my dress for a black one and I put on stout shoes and drew a black scarf over my head so that I'd be all but invisible in the darkness.

The evening was still young—not yet nine—but darkness had set in to its fullest. I made my way downstairs without meeting anyone, departed by the front door and went directly to the stables where I knew I would find a lantern. There were ample matches in the pocket of my dress.

Nearing the stables I heard voices, but they turned out to be those of the maids, the cook, and the hostler getting ready to return to their homes in the village, so I waited, concealed by shubbery, until the carriage rattled away.

I found a lantern, shook it to be sure it was well-filled with oil and then I walked resolutely in the direction of the chapel. This was going to require every bit of courage I possessed. In fact, I wasn't even certain I was brave enough to go through with it, but I did intend to try.

Approaching the chapel with a lighted lantern would be too much like announcing my presence, so I made my cautious way to the approach to the chapel. By this time I was familiar enough with the grounds to know when I reached the proper path and I was careful not to entangle myself on the brush. There was no moon, not even stars and I thought, at dusk, there'd been a hint of a storm, all of which suited me well—my prowling about must be done in the strictest secrecy, or I might place myself in deadly danger.

The chapel began to take shape out of the darkness and I paused to regard what was once a house of worship. In my opinion, someone had desecrated this peaceful edifice, turning it into a monstrous sideshow to no purpose that I knew of, or could possibly think of. The stained-glass windows were dark tonight, much to my relief, and the organ was silent. I turned away from it and, at that moment, I heard a slight movement to my left, the result of a branch being brushed against, and then came the crackle of dry twigs trampled upon by someone moving along off the path.

I looked about quickly for a place of refuge and selected a mighty oak with a trunk wide enough to conceal me. I stepped behind it, being careful not to let the lantern hit the bark.

Nothing further happened except that my heartbeat seemed loud enough to warn anyone away. The silence was, in fact, oppressive, but I didn't dare move, for that sound I'd heard was genuine.

Then I heard it again, a little closer at hand and, from where I stood looking down the path that ran beside the chapel and on to the family graveyard beyond, a figure moved warily out of the brush. A slim figure, and by the contour of the head, either hairless or wearing some covering that fitted snugly—like a stocking cap.

Billy Cornell! No question of it! While Bruce sought him in the village, he was here, probably to carry out some other weird command from whoever directed his efforts.

Billy had no idea anyone watched him. He'd been most careful in approaching the area of the chapel, but once there, since it seemed to be desolate, he was less careful. He walked on down the path now. In a few seconds he might vanish from my sight and I wanted to see where he was going.

My hiding place behind the tree was off the path so when I began to follow I trod only on soft grass. I had to move warily, lest I tread on a dry branch and thus betray my presence. Had Billy broken into a run, or even a fast walk, I might have lost him, but he appeared to be in no hurry.

Near the rear of the chapel, the path took a graceful curve toward the graveyard. Billy sauntered around this bend with me some distance behind him. Once around the bend, the path straightened out, but when I cleared the curve, Billy was no longer there. One moment I'd seen him; the next, he had mysteriously vanished. I recalled that he'd disappeared before.

I still didn't dare light the lantern and trying to discover where Billy had gone in this darkness was extremely difficult. If I blundered around, I'd make noise and likely be heard. I had no desire to meet this man face to face, for I considered him highly dangerous. The wisest course for me to follow, my common sense informed me, would be to wait until Bruce returned and take him into my confidence.

But I couldn't persuade myself. I had gone this far and there was no turning back. Besides, I had so little time left to unravel the mystery of what was going on here. Billy had disappeared. One moment I had a full view of him, the next he had vanished. How could he have managed such a thing? How could anyone, I asked myself? Then the answer came. We were behind the chapel. There must be a secret entrance. But where? And how did I go about finding it? I had to move cautiously so as not to alert Billy.

Then I saw the faintest glimmer of candlelight through

the thick leaves of a boxwood tree and my spirits rose. There *was* a secret passage into the chapel! And I had found it!

There were two such boxwood trees, growing very close together—thickly-branched trees through which it seemed nothing could penetrate save a small animal or a bird. Yet Billy had somehow gotten beyond them.

I was drawn by the candle flame and I moved up to the low trees and parted the branches carefully. A few feet ahead there was a narrow opening, though it was partially concealed by a large, though thin-limbed, branch. All I needed to do now was to move that branch aside, enter that aperture and perhaps the secret to Mystic Manor would be revealed.

I was eager to plunge ahead and see what lay beyond. Yet if I entered that place with Billy there, he would kill me. I knew it. He had been told to destroy me and I knew that idea would still be with him. For a moment I was filled with despair. Was I so close to the answer, only to be held back from discovering it by a simple-minded man whose brain had been poisoned against me?

Then my hopes rose. While I debated whether or not to throw caution to the winds and enter that place, the candle flame seemed to grow dimmer and dimmer—as if it was being moved further and further away from me, until it vanished altogether.

Summoning all my courage, I crawled through the space between the two boxwoods and there I found what I'd been looking for. I had entered some sort of cave with a gradual descent that seemed to proceed directly beneath the chapel itself. Now I knew I'd been right.

Moving down the gentle incline, I found myself in such intense darkness that I could go no further. Somewhere deeper in that gloom was Billy Cornell and my heart started to pound as fear assailed me. I was actually beginning to back out of the entrance when I heard the very soft sound of the organ.

Coming through this silence, reaching me here in some sort of cavern below the chapel, the low, repeated single note created in me the most intense kind of terror. My mouth even opened so that I might scream and relieve the pressure built up within me.

But I pressed my hand over it. I couldn't give way now. There was too much at stake. My brain, for once, functioned calmly, despite the sense of horror all about me. If Billy was in the chapel, up in the loft, then I must be quite alone here. It would certainly be safe to light my lantern and look about me to see where I really was.

I raised the lantern chimney glass, scraped a match, applied it to the wick and lowered the chimney in place. The flame was small at first, but soon began to grow and I turned it up somewhat.

The light served to steady me and I raised the lantern, held it high. Facing me were row upon row of wax dummies, lying side by side. There was a wooden surface here, a flooring, and everything seemed to be neat and tidy.

At the far end of the cavern, I saw a long bench. Here, undoubtedly, the waxen figures were manufactured. I moved toward it, my ears still assailed with the constant sound of the organ. There was no melody, only keys played at random. That, in itself, was evidence Billy didn't know how to play it. Immediately, I thought of Fern. She was an accomplished piano player. No doubt she was also skilled at the organ. Was it she who thought up this bizarre scheme to frighten me? Could these figures have been made so quickly? Faces which were so perfect they looked real? I doubted it.

However, I had no time now to speculate on it. I wanted to investigate this cavern and then, if my courage held, go upstairs and face Billy. Bruce had told me the man was cowardly. Perhaps, if I surprised him, he would not be so daring. And I knew I must see his face to learn if it was he who had attacked me. If his features bore scratches, I would have absolute proof.

Then, when Bruce returned, I'd bring him here and we'd at last solve this bizarre mystery.

I reached the bench. On it was some sort of turntable upon which the waxen heads were created. There was a head on it now and a wig lay alongside. A new figure must be in the process of being made. I hesitated to even touch that bald pate, but I chided myself for even hesitating at this stage. I lifted the lantern to see better and slowly turned the head around.

Why I didn't cry out in my fear, I'll never know. I should have, for the terror that ran through me was such that I almost dropped the lantern and fled. I was looking at my own image in wax. A perfect likeness, and the wig was

133

fashioned in the color of my hair and the way I customarily wore it.

I backed away in horror. I had seen the wax figures of four people up there in the chapel and all were dead. Was I scheduled to be next? Would my wax image join the others? Was I—a dead man's bride? Would my effigy be placed beside that of Vincent Seaton?

Frantically, I looked about, sending the light of the lantern in all directions, and there it stood—the headless image of a woman already wearing a wedding gown. All that was needed was the head beside me and a wedding veil to complete the effigy. And it would also complete the grisly tableau which would be set up in the chapel above.

Forcing myself to look closer, I studied the waxen head. There was something familiar about it. Of course, it was the duplicate of my own features and thus should have been familiar, but this was special. This was the expression created in wax which was a duplicate of the expression Bruce had put on canvas.

This time a cry of agony escaped me—all at once the answer had come. It was Bruce! The man I loved and trusted and had hoped to confide in when he returned from the village. He must be insane, I thought. First, painting his victims, then creating them in wax before he killed them.

My eyes filmed and I placed the lantern on the table beside the head and buried my face in my hands while I wept. How could I have been so mistaken in him? A man so gentle and kind—a murderer! I felt as if my life had suddenly ended. Was he coming back tonight to kill me? No doubt of it. Everyone would believe I had left for California. Everyone except Delphine. Was she aware of what he had done? Of this secret cave and entrance to the chapel? I had nowhere to go, no one to turn to and no escape from Mystic Manor.

The organ was still playing. One random note after another, no melody, just the low growl of the instrument. Billy, fiddling with the keys, amusing himself as he must have been accustomed to do, and had been doing the first night, when I saw the faint light through the stained-glass windows. His simple mind was likely fascinated by the instrument and the sounds he could create with it.

I was suddenly angry with him—angry also at myself for having been so completely fooled. So Bruce had gone to the village to find Billy, indeed! My smile was bitter as

I dried my tears. Anger overcame my fear and, perhaps, my caution, for I was determined to put an end to this myself by cornering Billy and making him tell the truth. Or, at least, learning if his face bore the marks of my fingernails, a small chore Bruce was supposed to have attended to, but never did seem able to catch up with. Poor, half-witted Billy.

I held the lantern higher and searched for the way into the chapel. I found it readily enough, about ten wooden steps that led to a door without a knob or latch, but which I could see by its outline. I climbed the stairs, tested it and one side moved inwards. It was merely set on some support around which it would revolve.

I came out in the rear of the chapel and the door closed behind me. I held the lantern close to what seemed to be solid wall, but I could not find the entrance to the cave. Not even when I pressed with the flat of my hand to make the section open. There was some trick to opening it from this side, but that wasn't important now. Billy Cornell was, and he still toyed with the organ.

I walked out to the altar and stood there, looking up at the loft where Billy sat at the organ. One of the tall candelabras beside the music rack was lit. Billy had his back to me and he was busy pumping the instrument with his feet while his fingers touched the keys which had so nearly frightened me out of my wits the first time I'd heard them.

I moved down the aisle, stepping softly, and still he didn't hear me, for even that low music filled the chapel. I wasn't afraid of him now. Perhaps he had tried to kill me, not only once but twice. If he turned on me now, I could still get away from him. I was as fleet of foot as he.

I went up the steep, narrow stairs to the loft, appearing quite suddenly close by the organ. With the lantern held level with my face, I must have presented a frightening picture to this thin-faced, blank-eyed little man. He was startled and gave a bleat of fear as he turned to face me. Now I saw the scratches on his face.

"You're the one," I said, and my voice was harsh with indignation. "You tried to kill me! Those are the marks of my nails."

"No! no!" he screamed. "No———"

He got up slowly from the organ bench. He was half crouched. I moved toward him and he backed away, just

135

as I was sure he would. Something brushed my shoulder and I glanced about. The bell rope hung at my side.

I stayed where I was. "Billy, I want the truth. You're going to tell it now. There's no one to protect you. Unless you tell the truth, the constable will come and take you. There's been murder done, more than once. You know what they do to people who kill others. Tell me the truth, Billy. If you do, I'll stand up for you. I'll help you."

"I don't know nothing," he pleaded. "All I do is come here and play the organ. I don't hurt nobody."

"You're lying, Billy."

"No I ain't. Honest, I ain't lying."

He had backed up as far as he could go and was touching the loft rail. I thought I could make him speak now, to tell me everything he knew about this, but I'd underestimated him. He may have been small, meek, scary, but he was cornered and he did what all animals do in that situation. He fought back. His right hand darted down to the half boots he was accustomed to wearing and from the top of one boot, he drew a knife. Now it was my turn to give way to fear. He moved a step forward and he was and dangerous as the bravest man alive. I had to do something to frighten or distract him. On impulse, I reached for the bell rope.

"Don't do that." he screamed at me. "Don't ring the bell! Somebody dies when the bell rings—don't ring it—oh, please——"

I pulled the rope as hard as I could. The ship's bell, much too large for this little chapel, gave a squeaky response. Then the clapper hit the bell and the first note went resounding out over the quiet countryside.

Here in the organ loft the sound was deafening. Billy screeched and threw away the knife to clap both hands to his ears, as if the sound was driving him mad.

I pulled the rope again and again and the bell clanged mightily. It could be heard all the way to the village. Let Bruce hear it. Let him realize that his plans had gone astray. Let him know the truth was coming out.

Billy, cowering there, hands hard against his ears, swayed back and forth in the agony the sound seemed to produce in him. Suddenly he screamed again and with one jump, hurtled over the organ rail down to the aisle below. It was a high jump and had he hit any of the pews, he would have surely broken a limb. But he landed in the aisle and though he lay there, shaken for a few seconds, he was up quickly enough and running like the wind for the chapel door.

I let go of the bell rope and suddenly I burst into tears. The tension had lifted, the danger was temporarily gone and, once again, the tears came, despite myself. Perhaps they were justified this time—the man to whom I'd given my heart was a bloody murderer.

He'd painted those young people whose effigies were in the cave below the chapel and each of them had died. Those whom he painted, he killed. So it seemed to me. He'd painted me and then from my likeness on canvas he had created a waxen image which would be part of his horrible tableau in the chapel.

The lantern swung listlessly from my hand as I stumbled down the loft steps. The chapel doors were wide open. I walked down the aisle slowly, as if the life had drained out of me. Nothing seemed to matter now. All I cherished was lost; perhaps my life would be sacrificed as well.

Someone was running swiftly down the path to the chapel. I didn't know who it was and I didn't care. For all I knew, it might be Bruce. I hoped it was. I kept on going so we'd meet as soon as possible. If he wanted to kill me, let him. I no longer cared about living—my courage had built on the love I thought he bore me.

TWELVE

"Melinda! Melinda!" Fern was calling my name. I raised the lantern in a signal that all was well, but she kept running toward me. When she finally reached my side, she was so out of breath that she couldn't speak.

"The bell," she finally was able to say. "Who rang the bell?"

"I did."

"But—what happened? Why?"

"Billy Cornell was in the chapel playing the organ. I tried to get him to speak, to tell me the truth of what's been going on here. There are things so horrible——"

"Billy? He's not there now?"

"He drew a knife and threatened to kill me. That's why I rang the bell. It seemed to drive him mad. He ran away——"

"Melinda, how horrible for you!" she exclaimed. "So it was Billy who killed Vincent Seaton."

It was on the tip of my tongue to dispute that—to tell her that it had been Bruce—but she was so obviously sincere, I could not. Before I made any accusation, I would bring the family to the chapel, show them what I'd discovered and see how they'd react.

Fern looked back over the path. "Delphine was following me. She should be here by now. The bell woke everyone. Tess pulled the covers over her head and refused to budge. Charity insisted on putting on a dress before she'd go outside—but Delphine. . . ."

I stopped her by raising my hand. I thought I'd heard a low moan, like someone not in pain, but filled with an overwhelming compassion. It came again, louder, and this time it was followed by a weak scream.

"That's Charity," Fern said. "In heaven's name, what's going to happen next!"

We both ran as fast as we could, I lighting the way with my swinging lantern. In my own heart was the dread that Billy Cornell had encountered Charity along the path. I breathed a sigh of relief as I saw her outlined before us like a wraith in the darkness. At her feet lay a form, quiet, ominously so. I reached the scene first. Charity seemed incapable of speech. She just stood there with both hands pressed tightly against her mouth, looking like a terrified child. I bent down to regard the still form.

"It's Delphine." I looked up at Fern who had reached my side. "She's alive, but very ill, I fear. We've got to get her into the house."

"She's dead," Charity said, uncovering her mouth. "My sister is dead! She's left me! She's dead——"

"No, Charity," I said. "She is not dead. Someone has to go to the village for Bruce——"

"No need for that," Fern said. "The chapel bell will bring him back." She raised Delphine's head slightly and we saw her eyelids flicker. "She's coming around."

Delphine's eyes opened all the way. She tried to say something, but no words came forth. She couldn't move a muscle. There was a heart-rending pleading in her eyes. I knew what was wrong.

"Fern, we must get her to the house and we can't carry her. Run to the stable and fetch a rig, a carriage, anything that you can drive over the lawn. Run as fast as you can. Please!"

Fern nodded obediently and began running as swiftly as she could. I placed the lantern on the ground, then raised Delphine slightly and supported her head shoulders on my lap. That was all I could do.

Charity stood looking down at us, trembling, her breath coming in gasps. I couldn't let her stand there any longer, for she was on the verge of hysteria.

"Run to the house and prepare your sister's bed. Make some tea. Throw an extra blanket on the bed. She must be kept warm."

Charity heard me, for I could see the understanding in her eyes, but she didn't move.

"Run!" I shouted. "Don't you want your sister to get well?"

She gave a slight gasp and ran off in the direction of the Manor House. I turned my attention to Delphine again. Her skin was cold to the touch and I began to rub her arms lightly while I kept up a constant chatter, partly to reassure her, partly for my own benefit.

"You'll be all right, Delphine. I think you fainted and you're very weak. Soon your strength will return. Bruce will be here soon too. The bell was heard in the village and he will know something's wrong. There is nothing to worry about. We'll get you in bed and have some hot tea—perhaps a little brandy for you. There's not a thing to fret about. . . ."

She closed her eyes once in a signal that she understood me, but I don't think she believed me and I didn't blame her. The time seemed endless. I was growing numb supporting Delphine's weight. I thought Fern would never return. But then, she would have to harness a horse to the rig, or whatever she would bring. She was likely no expert at it any more than I was.

About the time I really began to worry, I heard the sound of the vehicle and a buckboard came rocketing down the path, staying on all four wheels somehow. Fern pulled up the horse, jumped from the seat and we quickly lifted Delphine to the back where Fern thoughtfully placed several thick blankets. I climbed into the back with Delphine to hold her steady while Fern turned the rig around and held the horse to a trot on the way to the house.

I was worrying how we'd manage to carry her inside. She was not a small woman, nor a light-weight one. We'd had difficulty getting her into the back of the rig. However, our problem was settled for us by the arrival of Bruce, riding very hard.

"It's Delphine," I said. "She collapsed and she doesn't seem to be able to move."

"Get her bed ready," Bruce ordered brusquely. He touched Delphine's forehead and then, while I held the lantern, looked into her eyes. Next, he checked her pulse. Then he slipped his arms beneath her and carried her into the house.

Charity sat in one of the chairs in Delphine's room, weeping inconsolably. Fern had the bed ready and Bruce placed Delphine tenderly onto it. He glanced at Charity.

"Get her out of here," he ordered Fern. "Charity, go to your room. There is no danger. Your sister isn't going to die."

"Yes, she is," Charity said. "Yes, she is."

Nevertheless, Charity arose and Fern guided her from the room. Bruce paid scant heed to me. He was busy making Delphine comfortable and then examining her professionally. He sent me downstairs for his bag and, from it, he took some small white pills which he managed to get Delphine to swallow. Shortly thereafter, she closed her eyes and she seemed to relax. Bruce indicated I was to follow him and we went out into the corridor.

"She's had a stroke," he said. "I've been expecting it. Did something bring it on?"

"Yes. I was responsible, I'm afraid. I found Billy Cornell in the chapel. He was going to kill me and I rang the chapel bell to frighten him. It did, but it awoke everyone. Fern and Delphine were running to the chapel when Delphine collapsed."

"It wasn't your fault," he said.

"How bad is she?"

"It's hard to tell at this time. The damage seems quite severe, I'm afraid."

"Will she ever be able to talk or move again?"

"Talk, perhaps. Move? Some . . . if we're lucky. There may be a permanent paralysis. There almost always is. What made you go to the chapel?"

"Can't you guess?" I asked in a voice gone cold.

He looked at me strangely. "Guess what?"

"I discovered the place where the smugglers used to hide more of their contraband. It's in a cave beneath the chapel and there's a secret way into the chapel itself."

"I never knew," he marveled.

"There's no smuggler's contraband in the cave now. Only the wax effigies I saw in the church and the head of a new one, almost finished. Do you still claim ignorance?"

"What are you talking about?" he began, but from Delphine's bedroom came a low moan and Bruce left me to hurry to her side. I stood in the doorway. Apparently, Delphine was regaining the use of her voice to some extent for she was trying to whisper to him and Bruce had his ear close to her lips.

I turned and walked slowly away, my heart heavy at the thought of what I was about to do. I was going to prove his guilt and when I did, there'd be but one recourse for me. I'd have to escape the Manor, reach the village somehow and explain all the details to the constable. Though he'd very likely not believe a word I said—and I wouldn't blame him for that—I now had proof. He'd be duty bound to come here and investigate even the weird story I'd have to tell.

Bruce would be arrested. I'd be cleared of suspicion in the murder of Vincent Seaton and Bruce would be accused of the crime. Bruce, the man I'd fallen in love with, whose kisses and embraces I accepted eagerly, even hungrily, for I truly loved him. Could I now destroy him?

I thought of the others whom he'd painted, attended in death and then made wax images of. He was about to sacrifice me, and after me, there'd be others. He couldn't stop and I couldn't allow that to go on. Without further hesitation, I picked up a lamp from a table in the hall, went to the third floor and walked into the studio.

I used one of my supply of matches to light a lamp and I carried it to the easel. The portrait was covered as he'd left it. If I found the identical expression which was duplicated in wax, then I'd know it was Bruce beyond any doubt.

I raised the cloth cover and I retreated slowly from the portrait. It wasn't mine, but the one of Charity which he'd showed me. To me it was quite apparent what this meant. He'd been studying it, perhaps sketching it, so he might create poor Charity's image in wax also. She would, apparently, follow me in his fantastic scheming.

I looked about for my portrait and found it, face turned to the wall. I turned it so the lamplight would fall upon it and I saw the same expression I'd recognized on the waxen head. It was the blueprint for the wax image which would take my place after he killed me.

I had seen enough. I left the studio and returned to my rooms. I was numb with shock, but I sat down to think this out the best I could. The only conclusion I could arrive at was that Bruce must be totally mad. If so, he wasn't responsible for what had happened and so he would never be prosecuted. He would, instead, be confined and quite likely never set free again, but I'd continue to live and Charity would not be murdered. I wondered how many others were on his list.

Yet, no matter how hard I tried, I could not think of him as a madman. It seemed to me he'd have given some indication of it, no matter how slight, and Bruce was one of the steadiest men I had ever met. One of the wisest as well and, perhaps, I thought with a shudder, the cleverest. I'd told him of the cavern where the wax images were secreted. He knew very well that the truth was now evident to me. Therefore, my own danger was greater than ever. Still, I had to be absolutely certain. Even if it was at the risk of my life, I must be sure beyond the slightest doubt that Bruce was guilty of these crimes.

There was but one way to make certain of it. If I went to the cavern, concealed myself there and waited until he came, I could then watch his actions and have the positive proof. He was bound to visit the cavern as soon as he could possibly get away from Delphine without arousing suspicion, for he'd feel certain I'd take some action and he might have some place there where he could conceal the figures.

I was in an agony of indecision. How could I betray the man I loved as a wanton murderer? Yet if I remained here, I would be killed. I thought of packing a bag, taking the buckboard, which must still be outside, and making a dash for the village or even going beyond it to the nearest station on the railroad.

If I were to leave here, would Bruce pursue me? Or would he feel that, by my fleeing, I assured him of my silence regarding his guilt? I couldn't do it! There was Charity—and Fern who had thus far refused to sit for him. How wise of her, I thought.

But then question after question again began flooding my mind. How could I be certain it was he? Had I seen him make the wax figures? Did he know how to play the organ? Hadn't he told me, in intelligent fashion, that he'd never have been fooled by the bundle of clothes I'd fashioned, to make it appear I was in the bed and, of course, he would not. He swore innocence to any knowledge concerning the existence of a cave beneath the chapel. I realized I was doing the same thing to him that had been done to me in the village—pointing the finger of guilt, without one iota of proof.

If I ran away without being certain, I might be making a grave error. Others could have gained access to his studio and studied or sketched the paintings. It was possible that someone else was skilled enough to create these waxen images. There was no telling but that even poor, dull-witted Billy Cornell might be so gifted.

How did I know but that Delphine wasn't responsible for what had happened and she'd gone into shock when she realized I'd discovered the secret of the old chapel? Or it could be Fern. And even Mrs. Linton might have some well-hidden motive for such misdeeds and she had certainly been well able to carry on without being suspected.

There was a gentle knock on my door. I went to open it

and found myself facing Bruce. I suppose I must have looked startled and perhaps even frightened.

"What's the matter?" he asked.

"Oh—nothing. I—thought when I saw you that—Delphine had——"

"Delphine is still alive. May I come in and sit down?"

"Please do," I said, and I backed away from the door. He chose the padded rocker and lowered himself into it with a sigh. "Will you sit down or must I stand up again?"

"How is she?" I asked, easing myself onto the settee. I clasped my hands tightly in my lap to still their trembling.

"That's what I came to talk about. Fern is with her now. I'm afraid Delphine isn't going to live very long."

"Oh, Bruce," I said in dismay, forgetting my own fears in my compassion for the unfortunate woman.

"The stroke is a massive one. She may, of course, live for some time, but I'm beginning to doubt it."

"I'm sorry," I said. "I wish I could do something."

"You've done a great deal so far," he told me. "This is what I've been expecting and dreading. Now it's here and we have to do our best to save her, but in this sickness there is so little to be done. She's in no pain, however, which is a blessing."

"All because I rang the chapel bell in trying to save myself," I said dully.

"How could you know when this would happen? No one could. It isn't your fault, Melinda. Besides, your life was at stake. I must return to her soon. She is trying to speak and it may be she will find her voice again. But I had to talk to you. Tell me what you found at the chapel."

"Not now," I begged off."

He leaned forward and seized my hand. "I must know, Melinda."

"All I found was the entrance to the cavern below the chapel. It's between two large boxwoods. In the cavern are the wax images. That's all."

"What was Billy doing?"

"What he's likely been doing all along—trying to play the organ. It seems to fascinate him, but he can only play one note at a time and he plays very softly so that the music won't be heard any distance. He ran off. The chapel bell terrorized him and he fled. I don't think he'll be back."

"What else?" he demanded.

"Nothing. Nothing else, Bruce."

"No other person was present? You're not holding anything back?"

"I swear I saw no one else."

"Very well. I'll go back to Delphine now. You'd best get what rest you can. We all may need as much as we can get before this is over. I hope you won't leave now. Charity needs someone to look after her." His fingers holding my hand tightened. "I need you too, my darling. Don't forget that."

He arose and abruptly left the room. I didn't move for a long time and my mind dwelt on only one thing, how great was my love for this man. And if I loved him, I had to trust him, for reason told me trust was the most essential part of love; therefore, I must trust him no matter how dark the evidence. What I must do suddenly became clear to me. Everything had to be destroyed. The wax figures must never be seen by anyone else. Let the others believe I'd imagined them. I could bear that, but I could not bear the thought of Bruce being accused of murder.

I draped a cloak over my shoulders, left my rooms quietly and managed to walk past the closed door to Delphine's suite without being heard.

I was passing the door to Fern's rooms when I remembered two things. Charity had told me Fern knew how to fire a gun and possessed one. Secondly—Vincent Seaton had been shot, but the weapon used on him had never been accounted for. Fern was with Delphine, so Bruce had told me.

I tried her door and found it unlocked. Inside, a lamp burned low in the sitting room. I closed the door, looked in the bedroom to make sure I was quite alone and then I began to search for the gun. If Fern kept it for protection, she'd have it in a handy place so I began opening drawers quietly, but not until I examined the contents of the bedside table did I find it.

This was a heavy calibre six-gun with a long barrel. It lay on a folded towel in the drawer and had been carefully covered with another small towel. I picked up the gun gingerly for I disliked weapons of any sort. I could see the bullets in their chambers. I turned the cylinder and discovered one chamber was empty. I placed the tip of my finger against the muzzle of the gun and pushed hard enough so that some of the burned powder adhered to my flesh.

This gun had been fired not too long ago. A matter of several days, perhaps, but it could be the weapon that was used to kill Vincent Seaton. He'd been coming to see Fern. Charity had told me Fern had been jealous of me because Vincent had told her he loved me. Perhaps she'd been jealous of other girls Vincent had taken out. Could this jealously have led her to kill Vincent? Quite likely it could have, but how did a girl like Fern ever become involved with the creation of the wax images and all the rest of it?

She was talented, as was her brother, for she could play the piano. Therefore, she could probably play the organ as well. Certainly, someone who was skilled in the mechanics of it had offered an excellent rendition of the wedding march the night I'd been attracted to the chapel.

Fern! I found it hard to believe. She was so level-headed, so direct. Yet she could have stolen into Bruce's studio and copied the paintings for use in making the figures. The possibility was there, backed up now with this gun, recently fired. I did recall that it had been said the bullet responsible for Vincent's death had been a big one, from a big gun.

I placed the weapon back exactly as I'd found it and I left Fern's room as stealthily as I'd entered. I was more confused than ever, but my mind was still made up to go to the cavern beneath the chapel and destroy everything I found there.

THIRTEEN

I'd lost my lantern so I picked up a large table lamp, brimful of oil. Carrying this, I left the house and hurried to the chapel. I made up my mind to drag all the figures into the open and there saturate them with oil from the lamp and set them afire. In a matter of moments, the evidence would be gone forever.

With the figures, I'd also get rid of the equipment used to fashion the wax heads, the wigs, everything else used in this grim business. My common sense told me that someone in this house was guilty of Vincent's murder, but they'd been kind to me, regardless of their motive. Yet, I thought, was I committing a terrible wrong? Could I carry out this outlandish plan? A murderer was loose in this household and I was about to cover up all clues to his or her guilt. Yet I seemed to be driven to do it. My footsteps quickened lest my mind waver in its determination. I wondered if I was losing my mind. Was it fear driving me? Or was it love?

I came to the boxwoods, parted the branches as I'd done before, made my way through the opening and then walked down into the cavern itself. I stopped to light the lamp and then I had my first surprise. The figures were gone!

I moved quickly up to the workbench where my image had been in the process of being created. That was gone too and—in its place—to my sheer horror was the head of Charity. The expression, in Bruce's painting of her, had been perfectly captured. And the head was prepared, wig in place, coloring applied. I spun around, holding the lamp up to look for the headless image. It was nowhere in sight.

Above me, the chapel floor creaked. Someone was up there, setting the macabre stage, preparing that tableau of the wax wedding. I found a candle on the workbench, lit it and left it on the bench. It would provide enough light for me to climb the stairs. If it became necessary for me to blow out my lamp, I could do so without imperiling life and limb if I retreated.

I went up the steps quietly, pushed open the door a crack and peered out. I could see nothing, but the sound of activity was plainer. I needed something to prop the door open with, and there being nothing handy, I used the lamp. Stepping through, I placed the lamp so the door couldn't close.

I crossed the small space behind the altar and I could see faint light from the chapel itself. On tiptoe, I approached the altar and in the glow of candlelight, I saw the scene reset—the audience of silent figures, the three replicas of dead girls for the bridesmaids, the figure of the best man, also dead, and the groom, standing there so lifelike in the flickering light that had I not known what this was, I'd surely have believed it to be Vincent, alive and well.

There was but one change since the last time I'd looked upon this scene. Beside Vincent's figure stood the bride—a headless bride, but on the floor was piled up the yards of lace and cloth which would be the elaborate bridal veil when a head was provided for it to be placed upon. Then I realized there were four bridesmaids. Faintly I could make out the identity of the fourth one. It was my face!

And then I saw Billy Cornell. He was over his fright, for he was moving about, calmly arranging the tableau to suit himself—or following the instructions he'd been given by someone. He was completely preoccupied with what he was doing. I looked around to satisfy myself that there was no other living being in here.

I backed away from the scene and returned to the secret door. There was nothing I could do now. I'd had one encounter with Billy and been fortunate to escape with my life. I didn't want a second. I didn't know the meaning of what he did, nor why my place in the assembly was now that of a fourth bridesmaid. I didn't want to know. I wished only to get out of here as quickly as possible.

I made my way to the strange door, pulled it open and moved the darkened lamp aside so I could get through without upsetting it. Then I held the door wide and backed to the stairs leading to the cavern. I let the door close almost all the way before I bent to reach for my lamp, but my foot slipped off the stair landing and I almost went sprawling. In my efforts to save myself and be quiet in doing so, I let go of the door and it closed. The lamp was on the other side of it. I began pushing the door open to retrieve it when I heard voices. Not from the chapel, but distantly, as if someone approached the secret entrance to the cavern.

I moved down the steps as swiftly as possible, forgetting all about the lamp. I rushed to the bench where I'd left a candle burning and snuffed it with my fingers. Moving carefully, I made my way to the entrance of the cavern. The voices were quite close now. I reached the boxwoods and through the branches I could see the light from both a lantern and an oil lamp.

Bruce carried the lantern. Charity, clad in what seemed to be a flowing white gown, held the lamp and walked beside him. I was trapped in here. There was no way out unless I risked rushing past Billy, and there wasn't even time for that.

Bruce must be bringing Charity here to kill her. That thought struck me with a force that paralyzed my muscles as Delphine's shock had paralyzed her. I could only stand there, overwhelmed by the awfulness of the idea. Her head in wax was on the workbench, all ready to be placed on the shoulders of the headless bride upstairs. All was in readiness for whatever macabre ceremony was meant to follow the completion of the tableau.

Bruce entered the cavern first and the light of his lantern revealed me standing there immobile. Charity, who was directly behind him, also saw me. Without a word she came forward, carrying the lighted lamp. She went directly to the workbench and picked up the prepared replica of her own head. As if neither Bruce nor I even existed, she mounted the steps. I moved to intercept her and Bruce instantly grasped my arm, held me back. Charity pushed open the door and I heard it close behind her. I also heard something go rolling across the floor, stop and then roll again as if she'd kicked it. That would be the lamp I'd left there.

"She's mad," Bruce said in a whisper. "Up there—in the chapel—she's going to marry Vincent Seaton. Or her disordered mind believes she is."

"She . . . killed him?" I asked.

"Yes. I'll give you the details later. At this moment, she's harmless enough. She told me all about it. Her wax image will be the bride, standing beside Vincent. Charity will go to the organ loft and play the wedding march while poor, foolish Billy Cornell lights all the candles and opens the chapel doors. Just as you found it when you came upon the scene, only it wasn't quite complete. It was in the form of a rehearsal, but she was proud of it and wanted you to see it—because she likes you."

"Charity. . . . It was she all the time."

"All the time. We'll go up now. She won't mind. She

told me she was very happy that I could attend the wedding. We'll let her go through whatever motions she believes necessary and then we'll lead her away quietly."

"Oh, Bruce. Poor Charity. . . ."

"I suspected her madness, but not to this degree. Delphine told me."

I looked at him quickly. "She knew?"

"Yes. She was able to speak and told me everything. She's quite aware that she's not going to live long. The first thing she asked of me was to beg your forgiveness in her name."

"I'm bewildered," I said. "So many things have happened——"

"It's all finished now. We'll have to turn Charity over to the constable, but I'm sure that's only a formality. Will you help me with her?"

"Won't she resent me? There's a wax image of me up there. I'm one of the bridesmaids."

"It's a place of honor in her mind," he said.

"But Bruce—the other bridesmaids——"

"She killed them. She arranged with Billy to kill you, but she promised me she'd never do this again. She's mad but she speaks like someone quite sane. Come, we'd best get this over with."

Before we could take a step, we heard the notes of the organ boom out, this time in the beginning of the Wedding March. It made my blood run cold.

"Charity learned how to play long ago and she used to come to the chapel and practice on the organ," Bruce explained. "I'd forgotten about that and so had Fern. We were just children then."

We went up the stairs, I taking the lead for I knew the way. "There's a door which opens easily on this side, but it can't even be detected from inside the chapel, and there is no latch or knob—nothing, so we have to prop it open if we wish to return this way. I used my lamp."

"We'll leave by the main doors," he said.

I pushed open the secret door and at once the billow of smoke rushed over me and I cried out in fresh alarm. I hurriedly stepped into the space behind the altar. Bruce began to follow me.

"The door!" I screamed at him. "Don't let it close—we'll be trapped!"

I was barely in time, for the door was closing as Bruce

150

came through. He held it open. I seized an old chair I hadn't noticed before and used this as a door stop. Bruce and I then made our way through the increasing smoke to the altar.

We gazed upon a scene straight out of a nightmare. The chapel full of wax dummies, the principals in the wedding before the altar—they stood there silently, stiffly and fire was leaping from one figure to another. It was all so real I expected the figures to scream in pain. I could smell the oil and the flames were licking at the floor where it had spilled. Billy must have caused the fire by carelessly lighting the altar candles.

Already the flames were high enough to reach the ceiling and it was beginning to burn. In a matter of minutes, the entire interior of the chapel would be one wall of flames. Through them, we could see Charity in the loft, playing the organ, playing it louder and louder, all stops out, and it was no longer the Wedding March but an assembly of wild, shrieking notes. Billy stood beside the organ. Suddenly he began to pull at the chapel bell rope and that clanged out, adding to the cacophony of madness.

I pulled away from Bruce, intent on passing between the now furiously burning images so I could rush down the aisle and reach the loft to get Charity out of there.

Bruce sprinted after me, seized my arm. "You can't make it," he shouted above the din. "That's a solid wall of fire. We have to go in from the front door."

I knew that now, but I didn't move for a few seconds. I was morbidly fascinated by the sight of the images slowly melting and then taking fire. My own wax face was now distorted into a grotesque leer as if the figure enjoyed watching the horrible scene. Then the dress caught fire, the wig burned and the melting wax began to give off smoke before it too was consumed by the flame.

Bruce pushed me ahead of him. We rushed down the steps, across the secret cavern, out between the boxwoods, heedless of how the rough branches tore at our clothing and flesh. We raced around to the front of the chapel where the wide open doors revealed the hell inside.

Bruce left me and dashed into the chapel. I followed him, though I knew how dangerous it could be. We were able to reach a point about ten yards down the aisle, just beyond the organ loft. The organ was still playing furiously, but

151

the fire had reached the rafters and was descending rapidly toward the organ.

Billy was still pulling at the rope and screaming wildly. As if he realized his predicament for the first time, he let go of the rope and tried to go down the loft stairs. A rafter, burning end to end, fell from the ceiling and lodged on the stairs, instantly setting them on fire. Billy screeched his terror, rushed to the loft railing and vaulted it. This time he didn't land in the aisle, but directly on the pews. He disappeared between two rows of them as the ceiling began to fall on him.

The organ gave one more gasping surge of sound and then was quiet. I looked up, but Charity wasn't in sight. Apparently she'd slipped to the floor. We could do nothing. There was no way to reach her or Billy Cornell. We had, in fact, to flee for our own lives. Even so, Bruce was burned around the neck and face, and my own clothing caught fire so that I had to slap out the flames with my hands.

Bruce whisked me out of harm's way as the chapel roof broke into flames and started to fall. The walls would go next. The stained-glass windows were brilliant with color now, but only for seconds. They melted or exploded under the terrific heat.

Bruce put his arms around me and held me close. Inside, two people were by now dead. I found myself shivering in the horror of it all while Bruce whispered what comforting words he could summon.

We remained there a long time, it seemed. Until there were only embers and then, without a word, we turned and walked slowly away. There seemed to be a ghost-like silence over the estate, now that the mad sounds of death and destruction had subsided and vanished. I knew Fern would be beside herself with worry, but I also knew she wouldn't leave Delphine alone.

"Were you burned anywhere?" Bruce asked me.

"Slightly—my hands. It's nothing. Your face and neck——"

"Superficial," he said. "We got out of there before the heat really reached us. I suggest we return to the house and reassure Fern. Then I must tell you what and why. When I'm finished, I shall make arrangements for you to go away. That is, if you still wish to do so."

152

"I must first hear the story," I said. "Then I will make up my own mind."

He nodded understandingly. Wc reached the house and went on in.

FOURTEEN

Delphine lay with her eyes closed, her pallid face in repose. Bruce quickly apprised Fern of the death of Charity and Billy, and the destruction of the chapel. Fern's face tensed as she heard the story, but her eyes betrayed the horror she felt.

"Delphine has not opened her eyes since you left. She knows nothing of what happened and I thank heaven for that," Fern said.

Bruce nodded and bent over the stricken woman. Fern came to my side and put an arm about my waist. Without the utterance of a word we knew that the care, anxiety and terror of this night had brought us close. It had also ended all my doubts.

Bruce raised the bedcovers into place and joined us. "She's dying," he said. "Will you remain with her, Fern? Melinda and I will be downstairs. . . . Just call."

"I will," Fern agreed. She laid a supplicating hand on my arm. "Melinda, I beg of you to forgive me for the way I treated you. I did think you might be guilty of Vincent's murder."

"I ask your forgiveness also," I replied. "For I am guilty of the same sin. I thought you might have done it. Charity said you had a gun and knew how to use it."

"We'll begin anew," Fern said, her mouth twisted in a sad smile. "This time there will be neither fears nor doubts."

"Come with me," Bruce was urging me from the room. "I will explain everything to you. At least, all that I can."

Bruce carried his bag with him and in the dining room, where a silent and thoroughly frightened Mrs. Linton had lit every lamp and candle, we sat down while Bruce examined my hands. He gently treated them with an ointment and loosely wrapped them in gauze. While he worked, he talked.

"Charity's madness was not the kind that can readily be seen. Outwardly, she acted in a fairly normal manner, though her identities as both a girl and a grown woman were very evident. She must have discovered the cavern beneath the chapel a long time ago, and she used it as a studio in which to make her wax figures. It quite likely took her years, and she patterned each figure from someone she'd seen and been able to study so they all looked so lifelike. It wasn't until she had her congregation in satisfactory numbers that she began to conduct this campaign of murder."

"Oh, Bruce, did she really kill those people—the bridesmaids, the best man?"

"Yes. Quite cleverly too, so that even I, a doctor, wasn't aware of it beyond a mild suspicion that I couldn't develop to anything concrete. Those were the important people, the wedding party. She told me she'd even killed animals and made their images in wax."

"Bruce, was it she who killed Vincent? If so, let it go. . . ."

"While you continue to take the blame? Oh no—and we have the proof. Charity told me how, and why. Delphine also knew, and before Delphine lapsed into unconsciousness she had me write a statement which she signed. You are absolved completely."

I was astounded by this news, but there was more—much more.

"Vincent came here and courted Fern. I'm afraid she succumbed to his blandishments and fell in love with him, but when he discovered that Fern was not an heiress to this estate, he lost interest. He learned that Charity would one day have it all so he turned his attentions to her. Can you imagine what happened to Charity then? This handsome, suave-mannered man telling her she was beautiful, and vital, and how much he loved her? Poor Charity was so overcome that she finally boasted to him of her array of wax images and even took him to the cavern under the chapel and showed him the effigies of four people she confessed she had murdered."

"Vincent must have been shocked beyond words," I said.

"I can well imagine. But it didn't stop there. He told Charity that unless she gave him money, he would inform on her. Now that was Vincent's mistake, for he should have known Charity was mad and, to her, murder was not a crime, but merely a means to an end. She told me this. She agreed to give him a large sum if he would meet her in the cavern. He came to collect and she shot him with Fern's gun. Vincent managed to get out of the cavern, reach his horse and ride back to the village. He bled greatly on the way, but he was still alive when he reached your cottage

155

where he was found. Why he chose you to go to, I don't know. Let's be charitable and say when he boasted of his love for you, he meant it. He knew he was dying and wanted to be with you."

"Who was it robbed his body?"

"Billy Cornell. He brought the things he stole to Charity for, you see, Billy had been helping Charity in this mad scheme for months, perhaps years. Charity then hoped to prove your guilt by placing the articles in your rooms where they were bound to be found. She used the smuggler's tunnel to slip in and out of the house by night. She resented you because Vincent loved you."

"But Delphine," I exclaimed. "She knew . . . and yet she brought me here to Mystic Manor. Why?"

"Charity was her sister. She knew Charity had killed Vincent, for Charity told her. Like a little child proud of some deed, she went straight to Delphine and told her about it. Delphine put the gun back in Fern's room. Fern never even suspected it was her gun which killed Vincent. She hadn't looked at it in months."

"Yes, yes," I said with a touch of impatience, "but why did Delphine bring me here? I was the only suspect of the murder."

"Because she hoped, by doing so, Charity's guilt would never be uncovered. Delphine couldn't just offer you money to go away. You'd have been suspicious, and so would everyone else. So she pretended to have faith in your innocence, brought you here, and arranged for the tea party at which she knew very well how you'd be snubbed and hurt. That would then give her the excuse to advise you to go far away and she would loan you the money, even provide a job. If the tea party hadn't worked, there was still the dinner dance."

I lowered my eyes. "I suspected you," I said. "I'm ashamed to admit it, but that's the truth. I thought you painted those people and used the paintings to help you make the wax figures, for the likeness was so close. . . . I thought you were mad."

"Delphine told me Charity used to slip into my studio at night when we all slept. She was quite talented in sculpting, it seems. Delphine once had hopes she would be an artist, but the madness came first."

"The one person I never suspected was Charity," I said. "She was such a shy creature—so seemingly helpless."

"She had never grown up mentally. I was always concerned about her. Mainly, because she slept too much. One who spends hours sleeping during the day is either ill or stays up all night. Charity was not physically ill—and now we know she did stay up all night. That's when she worked on the images."

"It's tragic," I said. "If I'd only understood——"

"She tried to have you killed and yet you're sympathetic?"

"Of course. How could she know what she was doing? She even tried to throw suspicion on Fern."

He nodded. "And also on you by planting those items which Billy Cornell stole from Vincent's person, in your room."

"That really puzzled me," I admitted. "And, I suppose, it was Billy who tried to choke me and then stab me with the kitchen knife."

Bruce nodded. "I asked my aunt. She admitted it and pretended she had given Charity a sleeping potion so we wouldn't question her."

"The strain Delphine has been under was too much for her," I reasoned.

He shook his head slowly. "We'll probably never know all the answers. It's true, though, that Charity was obsessed with either getting you convicted of the crime, or murdered because of it. Charity's only excuse was that of madness. Delphine needs your forgiveness; she deliberately allowed you to be blamed for the murder Charity had committed. Delphine did, however, retain Attorney Todd to get you off, and made him swear he would never let this be known. He believed it to be an act of simple kindness on Delphine's part. It wasn't, of course. I hope you can forgive her."

"I do. Let us go to her side," I said. "If she regains consciousness, I shall tell her there is nothing to forgive. And I am not going away, Bruce. I don't know what your plans are, but whatever they are, I hope they can also be mine. I love you. I always did, even when I suspected you."

He bent forward and kissed my brow. Then his arm went around my waist and we walked upstairs to Delphine's room. Fern stood beside the bed and she gave us a slight smile, as if she knew all was well between us. Then the three of us sat down and began a vigil that was destined not to last very long.

FIFTEEN

Delphine died the next morning, quietly, and without knowing of the awful night that had been her last. The fire drew people from the village, of course, but they were told only that Charity and Billy were trapped in the flaming chapel and died there. Later, Bruce went to Attorney Todd with the full story and I was completely cleared of all suspicion.

A quiet investigation revealed how Charity became friendly with each of her victims when they were guests at the Manor, and how she had prevailed upon Bruce to paint their portraits. After that, using the paintings to guide her, she made wax images of the faces. Then, with the help of Billy Cornell, she killed them—so cleverly that murder was not even suspected.

Fern turned over the gun which Charity had used to kill Vincent so that there would be not the slightest doubt of my innocence. However, after all that had happened at Mystic Manor, Bruce and I decided we did not wish to live there—nor did Fern, I might add.

She carried out her threat to move to New York City and seek employment, and did so, even though, with Charity's death, she and Bruce became sole heirs to the estate. However, she is now happily married and has two children.

As for Bruce and me, we too moved to the city, where he has a fine practice. A year after our marriage I gave birth to a son and Bruce's pride warmed my heart. Now we have two daughters and another baby on the way and Bruce says it is time we moved out of our somewhat modest home, for it is insufficient for our needs. He has his eye on a Fifth Avenue mansion all the way uptown near Thirty-fifth Street. I'm rather frightened by the size and elegance of the abode, but Bruce says it is quite suitable for me and our family.

We never speak of Mystic Manor nor the terror-filled days I spent there. Once a year we go back to visit the cemetery. The charred remains of the burned-out chapel still stand, a gruesome reminder of the tragic end of Charity and Billy. Nor have we once set foot in the gloomy old mansion. Not even Mrs. Linton would stay there after Del-